D1036284

Sunset in the Lowcountry

MARGARET SIMONS

Sunset in the Lowcountry

BOHICKET

Charleston, SC
www.PalmettoPublishing.com

Sunset in the Lowcountry: Bohicket

Copyright © 2022 by Margaret Simons

All rights reserved

No portion of this book may be reproduced, stored in a retrieval system, or transmitted in any form by any means–electronic, mechanical, photocopy, recording, or other–except for brief quotations in printed reviews, without prior permission of the author.

First Edition

Hardcover ISBN: 978-1-68515-310-6
Paperback ISBN: 978-1-68515-311-3
eBook ISBN: 978-1-68515-312-0

Dedicated to all the
Chihuahuas
I have loved

Hades - Age 18

Contents

The Funeral

JUNE 2013

*S*he wanted to dance. To throw her arms up in the air and twirl around with joy. But instead she sat quietly until the director told her it was time for her to drop her rose into the grave. She stepped up and let the fresh flower float down to the very expensive mahogany-and-brass box. Then she stepped aside and watched as her daughters did the same, then the aunts, cousins, and what friends he had left. She clutched her hankie to her face to catch tears of happiness and to stifle her giggles. Rosie had thought this day would never come. She had thought she would die of terror before her husband ever met his maker.

Rosie and her daughters stayed at the little family plot, hidden from the country road by a row of trees, until the dirt and grass covered the hole in the ground and the thumper had pounded it all even and neat. Later, Rosie promised herself, she would come back with a box of salt and make an upside-down cross over his sorry ass. She never did that, but it was a good daydream for years to come.

1

When they were all back in Rosie's car, headed out for a big, expensive adventure, tears and laughter filled the car. Mother and daughters had loved and hated and mostly feared the dead man. Rosie was married to Roy for twenty-seven years. She met him through friends who never told her the James Dean lookalike was a mean drunk. She was so struck with lust and desire that she did not hear her family's warnings; she did not think about the fact that he guzzled alcohol from sunup to sundown. She was an inexperienced-in-love idiot, besotted with his slim body and his big puppy-dog eyes. After eight years and three babies, Rosie had begun to see the light.

"Where are you headed, Mom?" asked Star, the oldest child. "Let's go have some fun."

"Well," replied Rosie with a smirk in her voice, "since he left everything to that bald-headed sister of his, and I know she has not closed out his charge cards yet—I heard her tell her mother that she had to do that tomorrow with the lawyer—let's have some fun."

The women in the car cheered and tooted the car's horn.

Rosie wove her way through the streets of Charleston, and soon they were parked at the brand-new luxury hotel that had been built where the old, hated pink library had stood for decades.

"Oh Mama," breathed all three girls at the same time. This was the most beautiful place they had ever been.

"We need a suite with two baths," Rosie told the concierge without batting an eye. "Our luggage will arrive later tonight." With that and the almost-dead card, they were in heaven. "First we will have a bite and some wine at the bar."

After they were seated at a little table with a grand view down King Street, Rosie looked at her daughters and thought, *I don't know how you did it—you all are just wonderful in spite of the hell you grew up in.*

First there was Star. Rosie giggled to herself as she thought how she had named her children after her old dogs and Roy never even asked about it. Star was beautiful, with glossy brown hair and big blue eyes. In another year she would be a real veterinarian in Asheville. How that child had struggled!

Next there was Polly: short, chubby, bubbly, and the mother of two little male terrors. She had married right out of high school to get out of the horrible, painful conditions she had been born into. She was always busy and loved her blue-collar husband with abandon. She lived in Atlanta but often came for visits.

Then there was Izzy. *Oh, Izzy, I think she was born on speed*, thought Rosie. Izzy never stopped moving or

talking or making wild plans from which she often needed rescuing. Izzy had her degree from Clemson and then
joined the Peace Corps and was off to save poor children
in some forgotten piece of the world. *Oh, how I love them*,
Rosie thought. *How did they survive their childhoods? This
will probably be the last time we are all together...until
they come for my funeral.* Again, a quiet laugh to herself.

Roy Gatch's girls had a fairy-tale afternoon and night
on him. They shopped, they got their hair done, they
bought art, they dined like queens, they went to the hotel
spa. Exhausted, they flopped on the chairs in their suite
and looked at all they had bought. When it came time to
go to bed, these adult women engaged in a terrific pillow
fight about who was to sleep where. Like children they
screamed, ran around, and swung pillows with gusto. No
one wanted to sleep in the room with Rosie because she
snored like a steam engine. Finally Polly agreed to, as she
had some earbuds to help cancel out the snorts.

They settled down on Rosie's bed with their arms
about each other, shed a few tears for Roy, and promised
to help Rosie get her life back on track. Then each went to
her own bed and to sleep. A few feathers floated down to
land on the pretty shopping boxes that covered the floor.

The silk sheets felt like cool butter. Rosie folded her
arms under her head and began to think over the past

few days. She had some thank you notes to write. Late at night a week ago Roy had been drinking in his favorite bar, Big John's, since six o'clock that same night. Big John, who had retired from the New York Giants, was a warm, big-hearted, real-life giant. He had followed his dream and opened a small, very popular neighborhood bar in Charleston. He began to ease Roy out of the bar, as Roy was becoming a loud-mouthed pest.

"Come on, time to go, Slim." John had one arm around Roy's skinny waist and held the front door open with his other. Roy protested some, so John gave him a small push out. Roy angrily staggered across the old and cracked sidewalk, tripped on the uneven coping, and rolled into the street. People heard him scream and watched in horror as he tried to stand up, but he never saw the big white Jaguar. Mr. Beck had been going just a bit over the speed limit and listening to fifties CDs when all of a sudden his lights fell on something right in front of his grill. He hit the brakes hard but felt a sickening thud when his right tire crushed the life out of the drunken Roy.

The rest of the night had been filled with EMS personnel and police officers, who notified the family and took statements from the half-drunk people who had seen the accident. After a few days of speculative news stories, everything settled down. Following a lot of measuring of the distance between the door into Big John's and the street and interviewing the witnesses, the police determined John had done nothing wrong. Roy rolled into the street because he was drunk and he had stumbled. John's little push out the door had nothing to do with the gory accident. Mr. Beck had not been drinking or smoking or speeding excessively, and there was no way for him to have seen Roy.

The Gatch women had gathered at their home in Mount Pleasant, where they pretended to be very sad. Rosie got in touch with her mother and siblings to let them know what had happened. They were all very happy for her, as they had never liked Roy. In fact they had been frightened of the angry drunk and had no interest in even attending his funeral. They were supportive from a distance.

Yes, I must write that man a thank-you note, Rosie thought. Rosie had never met him, but she sure appreciated him. And that sweet, bald-headed sister-in-law, Dora. What a disgusting excuse for a human. She lived in New Jersey and had made one trip to Mount Pleasant in the twenty-seven years Rosie had been married to her brother. No calls, no presents for the girls, no letters. And that jerk had left her his life insurance and his pitiful little retirement check. Evil drunk. Rosie smiled a little because her daughters were now independent, and she had a pleasant little job and the drunk's social security benefits. Life would be OK. She sat up in bed and grabbed the half-full wine bottle from the bedside table, took a long drink, and settled back down.

Oh, she wished she could see Dora's face when she got this bill and the bill from the funeral home. Rosie and Dora had gone to the funeral home together to pick out a casket and arrange for a service. Rosie had made it very clear to the funeral director that she was not paying one cent for this affair. Dora had not heard Rosie, as she was sobbing loudly as she wandered among the many coffins. Not consulting Rosie, Dora claimed the most expensive box she saw. Rosie stayed quiet while Dora arranged for limousines to carry family members way out into the country for burial at an old family plot. Oh, her brother was to go in style. Rosie just smiled to herself, pulled the buttery sheets up higher, and fell into a deep, relaxing sleep.

What to Do? What to Do?

2014

*I*t took over a year to settle all Roy's debts and other paperwork. During that time Rosie cleared her house of every item that had to do with Roy. Clothes went to Habitat, along with his books and tools. His nasty, beat-up truck was sold. She even threw out the mattress and sheets they had slept on for years and years. The children had no interest in anything connected to Roy, but they had helped their mother clean house, coming and going throughout the year.

"It's done," said Rosie, as the three of them sat around the almost-bare living room. Izzy had left in March for her assignment in Ethiopia, so there were just Star and Polly for the final push of getting rid of Roy's things. "Who wants a snack?" Rosie went to the kitchen to fix a tray.

"What is Mother going to do?" asked Polly, her soft brown eyes filling with tears. "Who will help her? Who will take her to the doctor?" Tears rolled down her chubby cheeks. Even though the girls were talking quietly, Rosie could hear them through the half-closed kitchen door.

"Oh, come on, Polly," Star answered with a toss of her long brown hair. "You know Mom has some friends, church groups, and her job. She is only about fifty-one years old. Her health is good. She can have a good life. Maybe even a little wild fun. Who knows? But let's not worry before we have to. And you know, there is still Gee!"

"Oh God, Gee!" Polly wiped her face and giggled at the thought of Rosie's mother, whom they all called Gee. "That will sure keep her busy. Maybe they will get connecting rooms at the House of the Living Dead."

Ada, or Gee, as she was called when she became a grandmother, had never been an easy person. She had been born into a world just crawling out from the Civil War. Ada's family had lost everything in the war. Everything from plantations to self-respect. It was a gray world of lost dreams. A miasma of defeat filled everyone's brain. Therefore Ada's outlook on life was angry, dark, and suspicious. While Rosie had fought this dark cloud all her life, it made her easy prey for someone like the animal Roy Gatch.

"I heard that," said Rosie as she came through the door from the kitchen, bearing a huge tray of nibbles. She placed the tray on a table in the middle of the group. "I will not go to a nursing home and most definitely not one with my mother." That drew a big laugh.

Rosie poured them each a small glass of milk. "Maaaa, you know I don't drink milk," whined Polly. "And you can't make me, Maaaaa." It was an old family joke that had brought tears in past years but now brought gales of laughter. Rosie quickly removed the milk and whipped out a bottle of wine.

They drank and nibbled in silence for a few minutes. Then Rosie set her glass down and pulled out several pieces of heavy paper. "I want to paint the house. What colors do you like?" She slapped the color swatches on the table. "I want a beachy, clean look."

The girls exchanged looks. Star put her hand over Rosie's. "Mom, this is your house. We don't live here anymore, and we won't be back. Dad is gone. You gotta do this on your own. Pick what you want and like."

Rosie's face fell. "I never looked at it that way. What I want? What I like? I never have done that." Her voice trailed off as she pondered this new idea. To herself she thought, *By myself? That is lonely and scary. I can't do this by myself.* She quickly smiled and agreed that it would be a new adventure and a lot of fun. *Don't scare the children*, she told herself.

A few days later, Star and Polly both had to leave. Star was the newest doctor at an animal hospital in Asheville, so she could not be gone long. Her mind was already back with the sick puppies she had left under a tech's care. Polly's phone had rung every twenty minutes with pleas from home to settle this and that problem for her family. She had to get back to Atlanta. They stood in the driveway with their luggage packed. They hugged and kissed and made promises to call, to visit, to email. Rosie promised to call if she needed them. She told them she already had painters lined up. That was the first lie she had ever told her daughters. Rosie smiled and waved with vigor as her heart burst with agony, watching the cars leave her behind. Since Roy's death they had left Rosie alone several times, but always with the promise to return in a few weeks. But this time was for real, with no set dates to return.

Rosie stumbled up the steps and through her front door before she collapsed. She slowly sank to the floor and curled into the fetal position, sobbing, her face a rictus of pain. She could feel the whole universe whirling around her. What to do? What would she do for the next hundred years? *Oh, God help me, I have never been alone*, she thought. Rosie knew the Hag would be back. That dark voice in her head would expand and fill Rosie's life with dread and fear. *No*, Rosie cried, *oh God, keep her away.*

The Hag had found Rosie when she was only ten years old. Rosie was hiding under some bushes in the back yard, crying because her mother was in the house weeping over a pile of unpaid bills her deceased husband had left behind. Rosie really didn't understand why her mother was crying, but the Hag sure did. The evil, poisonous, dripping voice hissed in her ear: *You are poor now. You will be lucky to eat. You will have to give away your dog. Nobody loves you.* All the rest of her life, this cloud of noxious gas would rumble through her body. Every day, every event was a struggle with the Hag. A war in her head. The years with Roy had given the Hag a chance to really shine, but for some reason, Roy's death had closed her dragon lips. She would return, no doubt at all about that.

Then her cell phone rang. It jerked her back into the world, if not into reality. Out of habit, she pulled the cell from her back pocket and answered: "Hello." Her voice was raspy and hesitant.

"Are you OK?" It was her brother, William. "You sound like hell." William, twelve years older and many miles away, had not come to see her in several years, but he had been an invaluable help when it came to the legalities of Roy's death. She would not have survived those first months if not for his daily phone calls.

"Yes, I am OK. Star and Polly just left, and I am on the floor having a little cry. You know, it just hit me that I am alone. Really alone. And I don't know what to do."

"Well, first, get off the damn floor." Rosie stood up. "Now get a little glass of wine, and I will tell you what to do." She got a glass of wine from the sideboard and settled on the sofa. As he was older, and bossy, she always did as he said. And he was usually right. He sure had been about Roy, and she should have listened to him. Oh well, lust had won.

"First lose twenty pounds, put that dumpy house on the market, buy a little condo—no, first, come spend a few weeks up here with Sarah and me. We can help with the twenty pounds."

Damn, he never left her weight alone. He lived in Virginia with his sweet wife and three children. "I can't come for a visit, but the rest sounds good. My job has been very good about me taking time off when I needed it, but I need to get back on a steady calendar. Also I have altar duty this month, and I am supposed to host book club with Muff this month. And I am having lunch with Chick." Rosie's older sister, Chick, had returned to town from several months at her California home. She and Rosie had an on-and-off sisterly relationship.

"See?" William smiled into the phone. "What to do? What to do? You are doing it. You have a life. You are living. And you no longer have Roy to deal with. Glad Chick is back and you two are seeing each other."

Rosie was quiet for a minute. She sipped her wine as a small smile bloomed on her tear-streaked face. "Yes, Bro, you're right! Now tell me how to sell this house."

* * *

It took no more than four months for Rosie to sell her house and settle into a bright new condo on a small tidal creek. Real estate was hot in Mount Pleasant, and her house had been paid off years ago. She had done well. Chick had helped her with arranging the condo, especially hanging the artwork. Her girls were happy with the changes, and all three promised to come soon for a visit. She was back to regular work with the school system, she had visited her mother every Sunday, and she had gained three pounds.

Well, Rosie thought on a warm Saturday in October, *I better run up to the Pig and shop for the week*. The Big Pig was just a couple of miles from the condo. Rosie parked her little Escort and walked toward the grocery store. She noticed a group of people gathered on a patch of grass by the parking lot. She wandered over to see what they were looking at. *Oh my goodness, it's a pet adoption*, she thought. Rosie loved dogs, but Roy had forbidden any pets. "No fur, no feathers, no fins in my house," he had bellowed for twenty-seven years. *But Roy is gone*, she told herself, and she began to study the little faces in the cages.

It broke Rosie's heart to see so many unwanted animals. They knew they were unloved, each pair of eyes begging for a home. Rosie felt she had better leave quickly before the tears started to run down her face. But a little voice—it sounded like her Aunt Laura—spoke to her.

Please help me, please, Miss. Rosie looked around to find who had spoken to her, but no one was close to her or looking her way. *Please.* Rosie looked down into two round, pleading dark eyes. The little eyes were about to pop out of a tiny black face with two perfectly pointed ears and a button sized wet black nose.

"You talked to me?" Rosie almost laughed.

No, mind meld. Like Spock. My old owner loved Star Trek.

Oh my God, I am having a stroke! Rosie's hands flew to her head.

No, no, listen to me! No one but you can hear me. Don't ask why; I don't know. You must help me.

"You are cute, and I would love to have a dog. But..."

*This is my third trip to an adoption event. You only get four tries and then they, they...*the little voice choked.

"They what?" The little Chihuahua stood on her tiny hind feet and stretched her neck up tall as Rosie asked.

They put us in a big wire cage and dump the cage in the Cooper River. They drown us, because that is the cheapest way to get rid of us unwanted animals.

"No, oh my God, no!" Rosie shouted. Her shout brought an attendant on the run.

"May I help you? Is something wrong?" the young woman asked.

Rosie began speaking fast. "Yes. I want this dog right here. Right now." She pointed to the little black canine.

"Wonderful, wonderful. Bertha was on her last chance to get a home. This makes me so happy." She talked as she got the dog out of the cage and also produced a handful of papers for Rosie to fill out.

Rosie quickly filled out the papers, paid the adoption fee, and added a little more as a donation. She cuddled the dog up close to her face, covering her head with kisses. "You are safe now, Bertha." She was rewarded with several little dog kisses.

Walking across the parking lot, Rosie realized she had to get dog stuff. So she dropped the dog into her huge purse, covered her with a scarf, and headed to Walmart, which was right by the Pig. Bertha did not say a word but smiled to herself and dozed off.

Two hours later Rosie sat on her deck and took a big sip of wine. She had put up dog treats, dog food, dog piddle pads, and dog toys and placed two dog beds in the house, one by the sofa and one on the deck. Bertha sat in her lap.

"Bertha? Bertha?" Rosie asked in wonder. "How did you get that name?"

My owner was German and loved to pretend I was a Doberman, so he named me after the cannon, Big Bertha. He was a sweet old man. But he died and no one wanted me, so I was sent to the death chambers.

"Well, my little love, let's name you Hades because you were saved from hell today and today is almost Halloween. OK, it is not almost Halloween, but we can pretend. What do you think?"

Hell of a good name, Fräulein.

"I think what we have here is the beginning of a beautiful friendship, or something like that."

Rosie was excited to call everyone and announce the new addition to her household. Star and Polly were thrilled and wanted to meet their new little sister right then. Izzy could not be reached, as usual. Gee thought it was nice as long the dog stayed outdoors. Chick also said "nice" and "let me call you back." Her call to her brother lasted a long time, as he had some good news to tell her. His first remarks had concerned the dog's bathroom habits and fleas, however.

"You are going to like this. Jimmy, you know, who is in real estate, has been urging me to buy some property down on Seabrook."

Rosie knew Seabrook, as her church had a big camp on one end of the island. She had been to several retreats there and was aware of the beauty of the area. "OK, that sounds good."

"So I did. I took the bait," he said, and Rosie gasped in delight.

"Don't get your hopes up. I didn't buy a mansion. I got a small condo on the creek at this marina."

"This marina" ended up being Bohicket Marina, nestled close to Seabrook Island and Kiawah Island in the Low Country of South Carolina, south of Charleston. The marina bordered Bohicket Creek, an ancient tidal bowl where Indians used to fish and crab. Within a few miles, Bohicket Creek joined the dark, rippling Edisto River, and they flowed into the Atlantic Ocean. "Creek" was not the right word for Bohicket; it was more like a small river with a deep channel that attracted big sea creatures and yachts of all sizes from all over the world.

As a barrier island, Seabrook had withstood many hurricanes, invasions, fires, and developments. The Atlantic Ocean lapped the shore of the front of the island, and many creeks cut around Seabrook. Money had found the old island in the 1960s, so now it was packed with million-dollar homes, golf courses, and condos, but it had kept a little of its primitive personality. The old oak trees were covered in swaying gray moss; deer trotted around while alligators and snakes slithered wherever they wanted.

"Oh boy, oh boy." OK, not a mansion on a beachfront, but beggars cannot be choosers. William told her he and Sara were going to drive down to inspect what Jimmy had sold them, and he wanted Rosie to meet them there. Rosie happily agreed and wrote down the date.

Over the next few months, William made several trips down to his condo. Rosie was always pleased to join him. Rosie found the condo very comfortable. It had one bedroom with twin beds, a big living room facing the docks and creek, a neat kitchen and eating area also facing the water, and two bathrooms. The brick condo was snuggled into a short line of other condos and sheltered by huge oak trees. There was a small porch covered by the upstairs condo that made great shade but leaked badly when it rained or the occupant watered her plants. With the sofas pulled out and air mattresses blown up William figured it could sleep a dozen people. Sarah was not very happy as she was a mountain girl.

Once Chick came but had to leave shortly. William brought Gee out with her ten-ton wheelchair and all its stuff. She said, "It's nice. You can repaint, can't you? And why didn't you get more bedrooms?"

Christmas

2014

Rosie loved this car. After driving to work and into Charleston for years in a little old handed-down Ford thing that puffed and heaved over the long, high bridge that spanned the Cooper River, she thought the Taurus SHO was a dream. A touch of the pedal, and that huge V8 engine left other cars in the dust. In fact, Rosie had gotten her first and only speeding ticket in this wonderful car. With the moonroof open and the window down, Rosie now flew down I-526. It did not matter that the wind was cold; after all, it was December. Rosie's short reddish hair swirled about her round face and caused the little Chihuahua behind her neck to tuck her ears under her paws. There, just for a minute, Rosie felt eighteen, unburdened, free, and headed off on a wonderful but mysterious adventure. But Rosie was a long, long way past eighteen and carried an eighteen-wheeler full of burdens.

Brushing strands of hair off her glasses, Rosie determined to make the most of this last leg of the ride to the island. The Cooper River was sparkling under the bright sun, even if the marsh grasses were brown with winter colors. From the top of the bridge, she could see the Wando River coming down its ageless path that had supported tremendous rice plantations in the eighteenth and nineteenth centuries and before that had brought sustenance to the Indians. Now expensive modern neighborhoods were crawling their way out of the old Holy City and up the primitive banks of the dark river.

"Damn, dog, that is depressing. Look at that!" Rosie waved her hand out the car window in the direction of some new development in the distance. But the dog was too busy keeping her pointed ears out of the wind to reply. "OK, don't answer, you little old lady. But I refuse to be down. We are going to enjoy this trip no matter what." And she watched the speedometer jump from sixty to seventy.

That morning before she packed for the trip, Rosie had spent an hour with her therapist. Rosie had sought help for depression in every corner of her world—from friends, priests, doctors, groups, books. After all the hours of therapy and all the pills she had hopefully downed, Rosie had found her dog the best healer of hurt and sadness. A warm, furry snuggle gave more acceptance than any doctor and his prescription pad.

The only thing Rosie had learned in her search with doctors was a trick with a box. Dr. Boatwright had said to picture a pretty, small box. Or a large box. Make it plain or cover it with bright jewels. This is your box. In your mind, open and close it a few times. Really see it, feel it. Now, the doctor led her, think of an unpleasant person who makes you uncomfortable. Dr. Boatwright told her to close her eyes, open the box, and now push that bad person into the box. Push, cram, just get all of that person into the box. Slam the box and put it out of sight. After a few seconds, a bright, colorful light filled Rosie's mind; peace flowed into her brain. She bounded out of her chair to give the doctor a big hug. Dr. Boatwright told Rosie it was not a permanent fix; the box would slowly reopen, but it did give some relief. Rosie used the box trick often; sometimes it worked, and sometimes it did not. She kept it in the back pocket of her mind.

Thirty minutes later Rosie turned off Bohicket Road and into Bohicket Marina. After telling the Chihuahua to stay and putting the car into park, she heaved her heavy, stiff body out of the car and stretched. Standing by the car, Rosie could see the marsh behind the marina and the creek in front. She stepped to the keypad by the gate and quickly punched in the numbers 1512. Nothing. "Damn," she said to the pointed ears in the car window. She tried 1215. Nothing.

Well, double damn. Alone for the holidays, car full of stuff to be hauled into the condo, and what the hell was the gate number? Nothing to look forward to but eating and gaining a hundred pounds. Pounds. That was it! #1512. It worked, causing a happy swish sound. The big gate opened to let her drive into the complex.

It took twenty minutes to get the dog bed, heating pad, pillows, and bowls set up by the sliding doors. The food and clothes took another fifteen to store away. Then she mixed a vodka tonic with fresh lime and sat in the comfortable chair to take in the view. She loved the view. Could sit for hours and just look and look. The boat dock was just a few steps away from the front of the condo. Going off at right angles from the main dock were a dozen floating docks with slips for about ten boats on each side. A swift, deep tidal creek of dark water gave the boats a circuitous path to the sea on the other side of the island. The far side of the creek was lined with thick marsh grass that changed colors with the sun and with the seasons. Today the grass was dark brown, but the sky was a wonderful Carolina blue.

Usually there was a pleasant flow of men. Old, young, big, little, and sweaty men who hauled coolers and poles and other stuff to their boats in the morning and then staggered back up the dock in the dusk, looking triumphant, sunburned, and in need of a hot shower. There were usually women and children and always dogs, but she rarely noticed anything but the men and the dogs. It was neat to be a dirty old lady.

Today the whole area was surprisingly empty. No cars in the parking lot and no one on the docks. "I guess everyone is home for Christmas," she told the Chihuahua, who sat in her lap. The dog paid no attention to the remark but jumped to the floor and began to make nervous little circles at her feet. "Walk?"

Yes, yes, wagged the little black rat. *Hurry, hurry, got to sniff.*

"OK, here, let me put your collar on and out we go."

The little bundle of fur was a reason for Rosie to live. A reason to go to Walmart and buy food. A reason to get out of the house and walk down the street and chat with the neighbors.

In spite of the blue sky, the wind was icy cold, making it hard to lock the door. Rosie pulled the neck of her jacket up and pushed her hands into her pockets as she crossed the brick patio in two steps and then began to follow the dog's leash down the grass strip that ran parallel to the dock. The dog's lead was long so Hades could go this way and that. This made Hades happy because she could reach every blade of grass and pile of poo in sight before jerking to a stop when the lead ran out. Not even the freezing air could daunt the thrill of sticking her little black nose into every mound left in the grass by the handsome boat dogs that had passed that way. She made a pretty neat dirty old lady herself.

Rosie stepped onto the wooden dock, and Hades followed. The dog found it hard to walk on the horizontal boards because there was about an inch of space between each board. She learned to swing her little fanny so her hind feet came further forward and missed sliding into the cracks. It made Rosie smile to see the drunken gait propel the dog down the dock.

The condos that lined the dock all looked empty. They were pretty buildings, in keeping with the beautiful oak trees that dotted the lawns. A few of the condos' balconies were decorated with swags of green and well-placed red bows. A couple of Christmas trees winked out of windows. But Rosie and Hades were the only things out in the cold.

Hades stopped to give her full attention to a particularly old pile, so Rosie stood still and looked at the sky, which was beginning to turn orange as the light faded. The boat masts stood straight and dark against the sky. The marsh looked so dark as to be hiding evil in its mysterious folds. The cold, creeping evening settled on Rosie's heart, forcing her to remember why she was standing here, old, fat, and alone for the Christmas holidays.

Rosie had planned to spend the holidays with a girlfriend in Charleston who was also alone. They had planned to go to movies, shop and then attend midnight Christmas Eve services at old St. Michael's Episcopal Church in the city.

They would eat a lot and have a fairly pleasant time. They had made plans in October, when Rosie had learned her daughters would not be coming to Mount Pleasant for the December holidays. It would be lonely but not impossible.

Rosie had learned that life was a constant stream of change. Everything changed. From the men who said they loved you to the breasts that had once thrust proudly outward. It all changed. Sometimes very quickly, like a sudden speeding Jaguar, and often very slowly, like hips that just got bigger and bigger. Over the years Rosie had spent days sinking into the black depths of depression, screaming at the gods and demanding that her life be smooth. Her anger and pain drove all pleasure from her existence. Yet somewhere deep in her soul, a fire refused to die. It must have been the voice of her mother, who was a dreamer of big ideas for her children, or maybe it was the power of the blood inherited from generations of failures who nevertheless refused to succumb to the void. That little flame, fed by tons of Prozac, many bottles of red wine, and a little Zen, gave her the power to live and to enjoy living and to be damned determined to have a damned good time doing it.

So when Rosie's oldest daughter, Star, lovingly announced she would come home for the holidays so Mama would not be alone, Rosie changed the plans laid in October. Then just ten days before the holidays, Star got into a snit because Rosie had given an old boyfriend the phone number of new boyfriend's apartment where Star was staying. Daughter went ballistic and shouted she would not set foot in that town for Christmas. Rosie called the friend with whom she had made plans and then changed plans to see if the friend was still available. Nope, sorry, Friend replied, she was now headed out of town for the holidays. So Rosie was alone for Christmas.

Hades decided she was finished with that pile and tugged at her leash with surprising strength for a seven-pound dog. Rosie came back from her thoughts in time to hear, *I'm cold, I'm cold.*

Hades always repeated herself because she worried Rosie's busy mind would not hear her. They had "spoken" this way since Hades had come to live with Rosie. No one else could hear them. Rosie reached down to pat the tiny head and saw that the dog was shaking with cold.

"Come on, let's hurry," she said, and they dashed back up the dock and into the warm condo for another vodka and a can of liver mush.

The phone rang just as Rosie, with Hades curled in her lap, had settled into the big chair by the front glass doors now covered by soft curtains.

"Hello?"

"Did you have any trouble getting in?" William's deep male voice demanded.

"Hey, Bro. No, all is well and comfortable. Thank you for letting me have this place at the last minute." Rosie loved her brother and often thanked what gods there were for his life. "Hades and I are very warm and happy."

"Don't let that rat ruin my carpet," he rumbled. Rosie suppressed a laugh as she thought about his smelly, three hundred-pound Lab who thought nothing was as good as squiggling her scabby back all over the fairly new floor coverings.

"You know she uses her piddle pad," Rosie replied. "She is a lady."

"Don't have any wild parties," he ordered, and she thought, *I wish*. "What are you going to do?"

"Chick has asked me to go to a party with her tomorrow night, and then on Christmas, the two of us will go see the old lady. The rest of the time, I plan just to sit, cable surf, and watch for sweaty men on the dock. I should say shivering men."

"I'm sorry your plans got dashed. You two are good daughters to go see Mother. For a treat, walk up the dock to the little café and have an expensive meal on me."

She didn't tell him the café was closed until January 5.

"Take care. Be safe. Love," he said, and he was gone.

She dozed off and awoke with a jerk to the sound of a boat's horn. Hades was yapping with such gusto she lifted herself off her feet with each sharp bark.

What is it? What is it? the dog demanded.

Rosie parted the curtains just a bit so she could look up and down the dock. It was as dark as a witch's eye. The horn blared again, and so did the dog. Rosie turned off the table lamp and opened the curtains wider. After a few seconds, her eyes adjusted, and she could make out a boat attempting to dock at the floating dock right in front of the condo.

The boat was about thirty feet long with two masts and a cabin. Rosie could barely make out the shape in the dark. The tide was rushing out of the creek, making it very difficult for the captain to maneuver in the swirling water. Each time the boat seemed lined up with the slip, the stern would whip to the left with the tide. After watching for several minutes, curious Rosie opened the sliding door and stepped outside into the damp, freezing night so she could see better. What else was there to do? Hades just stuck her nose out and then quickly retreated into the warmth. Rosie closed the door but remained outside.

Rosie stood in the shadow of the upstairs condo's porch and enjoyed the show. The boat went up and back.

The captain bellowed curses and threw lines here and there. Finally the boat was tied to the dock, and the captain continued to curse the creek, the tide, the cold, the dark, and Goddamn it, he wanted a beer. By this time Rosie was laughing out loud. She watched as the captain stamped his way up the dock. He was of medium height, bearded, and preceded by a magnificent belly. That was all she could see in the dark. He carried something on his left arm.

He walked straight toward Rosie. She stepped back into deeper shadows so he would not see her. She still laughed softly. He came off the dock and onto the grassy strip right in front of where she was hidden by shadows. He bent over with more muttered curses and put something down. Rosie had to strain to make out what he had set down. It moved. It yapped. Hades yapped and stuck her little face under the curtain so she could see. Hades smiled.

It's a Chihuahua. The mighty captain of curses has a little, tiny Chihuahua. Rosie had to cram her hand into her mouth so as not to shout with laughter, but she remained quiet. The dog squatted and the man unzipped, and they both watered the cold grass.

"Oh God," Rosie hooted. She was overcome with loud, snorting laughter.

"What th—" The captain spun around, almost dousing her with his stream.

"Oh God" was all Rosie could manage. "You are better than cable!"

The dog had recovered quickly and dashed to the door to rub noses and yap with Hades through the glass, but the man, with his cold hands, was having trouble getting things stopped and back into place.

"Shit. It snagged on the zipper." His hands flapped in the cold night air as he danced in pain. "Where did you come from? Who are you? I can't see you." He lurched around, still fiddling with his fly. "Oh, it hurts! Damn. What to do? It's snagged. Snagged!" His voice climbed with each utterance. With his back to Rosie, he struggled, whimpered, and finally grew still.

"Stay here." Rosie giggled. She quickly opened the door wide enough to slip through and raced to the fridge and grabbed a six-pack of beer.

She pushed her arm with the beer back out of the door and said, "Here. This is for the entertainment." And then she closed and locked the door.

"Thanks, whoever you are," he replied to the dark, curtained door. "I need this." With that he picked up his boat rat and went back down the slanting ramp to his slip, walking with a hitch in his step and his head lowered.

Rosie and Hades slept well that night, exhausted from laughing and sniffing. What was better than a good belly laugh? Nothing, Rosie had decided long ago.

* * *

The next afternoon Rosie and Hades drove into the old city of Charleston. What luck to find a parking space on that narrow old street. All the residents fought over the spaces; visitors often had to draw blood to get a spot. Or they could park on the beautiful Battery, right by the harbor, and walk back up Legare.

"Good luck—right here in front of the house," Rosie said to the rat.

Hades didn't say a word. She just looked up and down the street. Then she whined, *Where is the dirt, the dirt? I don't see any dirt.*

"You are in the Holy City, old girl," Rosie told her. "Here, get into your carrier."

Rosie's sister, Chick, had married well, divorced even better, recovered, and was enjoying a life of interesting, artistic people. Chick had an abundance of talent. She danced, painted, wrote, and advised others with abandon. She had homes on both sides of the continent but liked California the best because of the flow of new, if somewhat strange, ideas that constantly swept the West Coast.

Chick's house in Charleston was over two hundred years old. It was brick, three stories, with beautiful verandas running down the side of the house on all three floors. The lot was long and narrow, as was common in the historic part of town. She bought the house many years ago when the market for such homes was low, but now the house was worth a zillion dollars. The rooms were huge, with high ceilings decorated by detailed slave-carved moldings. The dark floors were covered with Persian rugs that had been collected over the years. Antiques from ages past stood at attention against the old, plastered walls. The house had survived many crises: wars, divorces, deaths, upheavals, earthquakes, and hurricanes. Just over a decade ago, Hurricane Hugo had slimed the first floor with thick, gooey mud and caused rain to come through the roof and threaten the beautiful plaster.

But the house survived. It often was on the city's historical tours. People loved to climb the long staircase with its wide, dark banister that connected the first floor to the second floor, where the big, open rooms were. But the public never got to spend the night in the beautiful third-floor bedrooms under a generous canopy; never got to use the old, old bathrooms with the knocking pipes; never got to undress in rooms cold as a witch's behind, where the lights went off and on with ghostly abandon. The awestruck public never had the opportunity to cook in the kitchen from the Dark Ages. They just saw the romantic rooms that had served as a stage for some scenes in the miniseries *North and South*. Chick never could decide whether to put money into that house or buy a bigger place in California. So she did neither.

Rosie pushed open the tall iron gate and crossed the path to the front door. She lifted the heavy brass knocker and let it fall.

I'm cold, I'm cold came from the carrier. The door swung open, and Chick welcomed Rosie with open arms and a big "Dahling! Come in, come on in. Let me take the carrier."

No. Don't let her, don't let her. I'll yell. The carrier began to jerk in Rosie's hand.

"I better take it. Here, you can take this bag." Rosie knew Hades remembered the last visit here, when Chick banged her carrier against the door and made the little dog squeal.

Chick took the suitcase and led the way upstairs. Rosie waddled behind her older sister's trim, tight little body. She might have been sixty-five years old, but damn, she looked better than Rosie had ever looked. They arrived at the top of the stairs, with Rosie panting and Chick chatting away.

"Put your things here, and we will take them to the third floor later."

"Thank God," Rosie gasped and followed Chick through the cold, softly lit drawing room, into the dining room with all the old silver, and on into the back den, where there was some hint of heat. She put the carrier down and sat on the sofa.

Cat. I smell cat. I smell a cat. Let me out. A small nostril flared through the little door of the carrier. Rosie opened it, and Hades ran full tilt out into the friendly room and began to search for the cat that was outside. This was very lucky for Hades, because the cat outweighed her by ten pounds and packed a set of killer claws.

Hades had a healthy sense of self. She challenged everything from pit bulls to kids on bikes. After all, the postman had never gotten into her home! Each morning she drove him away by throwing her small body at the window by the mailbox and hurling threats of damnation at him through exposed fangs. Hades did not fear a mere cat. After all she had been brought up to think she was a Doberman.

"Don't let that rat ruin my rugs," Chick ordered, and Rosie wondered whether her brother and sister had consulted each other in regard to Hades's habits. "Want a glass of wine?"

Chick never settled in one spot but always moved around, staying busy at this and that. Maybe that was how she remained so svelte. Today she was making new book covers for the millions of old volumes that lined the walls in the den and overflowed into other rooms as well. There was a roll of brown paper and a roll of clear plastic. She was lettering the brown cover, drawing an appropriate illustration, and then finishing it off with a clear jacket. The ones she had finished gleamed and gave the old, dusty bookshelves a bit of new pizzazz.

"She won't hurt your rugs. Will you, Hades?"

Hades just grinned and continued her search for the cat.

"And yes to the wine."

A couple of hours later, the trio climbed the long staircase to the cold third floor. *Damn, is this a mountain?* Hades's toes tap-tapped on the wooden steps. "Hush," said Rosie. "Act like you have some couth."

The room was so dark that Chick had to direct Rosie to turn on a dresser lamp that could barely be seen: "Keep going, reach to your left. A little more."

Rosie waved her hand around in the dark till it touched a switch button on the base of what she assumed was the lamp. But instead of warm light, a raucous voice broke into a shrill rendition of "Jingle Bells." Hades yapped and raced under the bed. Rosie screamed, stumbled backward, and tripped, falling on the bed. The thing still sang with gusto and then began to dance.

"Shit! Damn! What is that?" Rosie gasped, her heart thudding in her chest.

Chick had to grab the doorframe to keep from falling, she was laughing so hard. Tears ran down her face.

"You did it again!" Rosie roared. "You always get a thrill out of scaring the shit out of me." Rosie sat up and moved toward the dresser again, and again the thing, which she made out to be a small Christmas tree with big eyes and a wide, moving mouth, began to entertain. Once more, Rosie screamed but then began to laugh. The sisters had a wonderful dark humor that had seen them through situations that would have destroyed most women. They hooted some more and made the tree sing several more times till they ached from laughing.

"Get ready, and I'll meet you downstairs," Chick directed when she could speak, and then she went to her room to dress.

Rosie put the carrier in the small bathroom joined to the bedroom and plugged in Hades's heating pad. With a water dish, dog food on a magazine page, and a piddle pad, the little dog accepted the fact that she was going to be left alone and curled up on the warm pad to dream of finding that cat and ridding the world of another mewing menace.

Rosie freshened her makeup. She wore a black knit long-sleeve top and black pants. She put on several silver bracelets and hung a cluster of Christmas bells with colorful doodads around her neck. Then she pulled on a black jacket and slid a long red scarf around her collar. Getting dressed to go to a party of the social elite was a daunting task. What does an overweight, single, small-town, fifty-seven-year-old widow wear to a party in the big city? She looked into the old, spotty mirror. She turned this way and that, but there was no hope of not seeing the pudgy, middle-aged shape. No way to keep the stomach tucked in and the boobs thrust out.

To hell with all that. Just relax and be nice, nice, observed Hades from her pad. *Don't be late or I'll yell, I'll yell. Have a good time*, she added.

Going down steps was difficult with heels and bifocals, so Rosie descended slowly to the long-shadowed hall. She walked into the chilly drawing room and made herself as comfortable as possible on the stiff sofa. OK, Rosie pondered to herself, this room had served as a setting for the television miniseries which people all over the country had seen, but it was still a cold, stark room when the fire was not lit and it was not full of people.

Chick swept into the room wearing a form-fitting outfit topped off with a colorful, exotic wrap.

"You are in black again. You ought to wear more color. I will get you a scarf with some life." And she left to fetch another colorful, exotic wrap that she placed around Rosie while removing the scorned little red thing Rosie had worn. "There. Now you look better." In the past something like this would have crushed and angered Rosie. She would have spent hours resenting her sister's remarks but at the same time being jealous of her fashion sense. Time had taught her that Chick did have more fashion sense than she did. Also Rosie liked the attention; she was glad someone cared what she wore.

Chick served them both white wine in beautiful, long-stemmed crystal glasses. After finishing the drinks and taking a quick adjustment glance in the huge floor-to-ceiling hall mirror, the two women dashed down the stairs and into the cold night and quickly got into Chick's car. Chick drove the world's biggest Mercedes—silver, huge, and old.

Chick sped through the Holy City to a narrow street above Broad Street and began to search for the elusive parking spot. She spotted one in front of the house where the party was but could not wiggle into it. Then she zoomed down and across the street only to find the empty space guarded by a fire hydrant. She jerked the car into reverse and shot back up the street and around a corner to a nice, safe little spot.

"Thank you, Lord," prayed Rosie, because Chick had accomplished parking while touching up her lips and cursing all the politicians who had grown fat-cat rich from overselling the old city to rich northerners who thought it was cute to own a house in the city where Rhett Butler had lived.

The result was this mess of crowded streets lined with trendy shops filled with scented candles and other pricey items no local resident needed or wanted. The locals preferred their old city as it had been since the Civil War. They liked the miasma of noble lost causes and mossy dreams of past wealth produced by the labor of devoted, loving black slaves. The fact that over half of the city had been almost starving because there were no jobs in that mausoleum to the past was not their problem. Now with a progressive mayor and a ton of courting the tourist trade, people worked, and money poured into many pockets, but there was nowhere to park!

An hour later Rosie was into her second glass of merlot and surveying the people gathered at the party. No matter how hard she tried, there was always that nasty little voice in her head that no amount of Prozac or Zen could kill. That nasty voice constantly spewed forth vile comparisons of herself to everyone else in sight. She had learned to turn a deaf ear to the evil mutterings, but events like being deserted for Christmas made her susceptible. The voice, which for some reason had been quiet for several days, was in full form tonight.

Ha, the voice grated. *Where is your little dog? Gotcha, haven't I?*

Shut up, Rosie told the Hag.

No, I won't. Look around. You outweigh everyone here, including the men, by at least fifty pounds. And who is eating? Not that skinny person. You are! That woman is a CBS reporter, that man does casting for movies, and the hostess painted these beautiful walls and has a filthy rich husband. Over there is a book editor. What are you? A retired teacher. Ha Ha.

Shut up. I look good. I'm friendly. I've made good conversation with all of them. They are nice people.

Then why are you standing alone eating? Stupid!

For a moment Rosie frowned and considered giving in to the Hag in her head and running into the night, running to oblivion. But that would take more energy than Rosie had. Besides, giving in to a screaming, full-fledged breakdown was reserved only for the very rich, who could afford them, or for the very poor, who never paid their own bills anyway. The working middle class could not afford the luxury.

Rosie fought back. *The food is good, and I am hungry, you Hag. Shut up.* Rosie's right hand stopped halfway to her mouth. She studied the tiny cracker with a smear of something green on it. She gave the Hag's question some thought. She ate because it felt good. There had always been enough food at home, but her mother had never kept cookies or chips or anything unnecessary. Being full of sugar, a little grease, and a lot of butter made her feel comforted and safe. When anything went wrong, she grabbed something to eat. Once her neighbor's house had caught on fire. Rosie had watched the fire while eating a peanut butter sandwich. A candy bar before a test at school had been a sneaky must. If someone put a plate of food in front of her, she ate it all, not just a dainty, ladylike portion. Rosie just flat-out loved to eat. Eating was better than Prozac.

Someone spoke to Rosie, and she immediately became engaged in a cheery conversation that drove the Hag back into her cave for the rest of the evening. But not forever, never forever. The talk was light, interesting. People flowed around the rooms spreading warmth and gossip. After a while Chick appeared in her slim, eggplant-colored outfit, dramatically threw her wrap around her shoulders, and took Rosie by the hand. They said thank you and goodbye, and they made their way home to the tall brick house.

Snuggled under a mound of covers, Rosie stroked Hades' head. The sleepy dog raised her ears.

Was the Hag there?

"Yes, she always knows when you're not with me."

One day I'll kill her. I will. The dog moved even closer to Rosie's body and pushed her cold, tiny nose against Rosie's hand. *I love you.*

"I love you, too, little one. Good night."

* * *

Rosie and Hades were glad to get back to the warm condo by the creek by midafternoon the next day. The complex was still deserted. The boats rocked gently with the tide. The riggings made sharp noises as they slapped against the masts. Rosie had opened the curtains to the glass sliding doors but saw no one in sight. She settled into the chair and began to cable surf as Hades dozed on the heating pad. It was Christmas Eve, and all she had to look forward to for this lonely Christmas Day was a visit with her sister to the old folks' home where their mother was an inmate. She would meet Chick at the home about noon the next day.

Rosie lost herself in an old black-and-white film noir until Hades began to stir at about dusk. Hades stretched her front legs out and placed her head between her paws with her rump raised in the air. Her eyes sparkled, and her thin tail made quick little waves back and forth.

Walk, walk! she shouted.

Rosie, being well trained, put the dog's collar on her and a coat on herself and slid the door back. When she stepped outside, she saw a neat pile of six empty beer cans that had been placed beside the door. A piece of paper was sticking out of one of the cans. She reached down for the paper and read what was on it.

Thanks. More? 7:00?

Rosie's stomach gave a little lurch. She was thrilled. A mystery man. This would be fun. Hades had stretched her leash till she was behind a bush and busily deciphering a new pile of poo.

Forget it, fatty. You are just setting yourself up. No one is interested in a slob like you. Didn't your own sister tell you so? The Hag was back. *He has a bimbo on the boat and is only after free beer, sucker.*

"Shut up," Rosie said out loud without knowing it. "Shut up."

Hades heard this and dashed around the bush to see who she had missed. It took her but a second to realize the Hag had barged into their walk. Rosie stood with a piece of paper in her hand, beer cans at her feet, and a sad, defeated expression on her face.

I'll kill her, I'll kill her. Whatever she said, she is wrong, wrong. The little body jumped up and down and took off down the strip of grass. Rosie was forced to follow. The movement made Rosie feel better, and she read the note again. *Why not? Go for it. Nothing can happen that has not crushed you before*, she told herself. *Just enjoy. Don't let the Hag get you down.*

As Rosie followed Hades from sniff to sniff, she looked at the beauty around her. The graceful trees. The swaying moss on the tree limbs. The undulating waters. Beautiful birds swooping through the sky. Tall marsh grass swaying by the edge of the pluff mud. The air was sharp with salt and earthy aromas. It was a place of beauty. A place to put aside fears and worries. A place to enjoy life.

"Come on, little dog. Time for a drink and a page of dog food." Hades never ate out of a bowl. She did not like the clink her teeth made on the hard surface. She really liked a page from a magazine.

Rosie and the dog bustled around the condo. By 6:30 p.m., supper was over and cleaned up. Rosie had debated with herself over how prepared to be for the seven o'clock visit. Get all fixed up—or do nothing? She settled on old jeans with a bright sweater, clean teeth, and a little makeup.

Go for the relaxed look. Is his dog coming?

"I don't know, but straighten up your doggy playthings anyway," Rosie replied.

Hades looked at her with wide eyes. *Me work? Work? Are you nuts?*

"OK, I'll pick up your toys," Rosie said as she moved around putting things back into place and pushing the heating pad out of sight into the dog carrier.

By 6:45 p.m., Rosie was in the chair doing her best not to be excited. *I'm cool. I'm cool*, she told herself.

Liar, liar, echoed Hades.

Fool, fool, muttered the Hag.

"Shut up, both of you," said Rosie as she began to channel surf. She found *Lawrence of Arabia. Wow*, thought Rosie, *two good men in one night*, and she began to watch the TV.

At 7:10 p.m., the Hag said, *I told you so.*

Shut up came the reply from both Hades and Rosie.

I'll kill you came from Hades.

There was a loud rap on the glass door. Both Rosie and Hades jumped. Hades yapped at the top of her lungs, and Rosie slid open the door.

"Come in," she said to the large man holding the tiny dog.

Come in, come in, it's cold.

Rosie felt awkward as the man came in and began to shed his jacket and kick his sandals off. He put his tiny bundle down, and they watched as the two Chihuahuas looked each other over. Neither little animal could remember ever seeing another dog so small.

"What's her name?" Rosie asked.

"Jigger," he replied.

Hades stood still as Jigger greeted her rear. Then Hades gave Jigger a quick sniff. *Let's play!*

And Hades streaked from the room with Jigger on her heels. They both yapped with glee.

Rosie was not sure what to do. She wished breaking the ice with the strange man was as easy as the way the two pups greeted each other.

"Have a seat." She motioned to the sofa. "Have a beer?" She moved to the fridge, feeling a little scared of this huge, unknown bearded person. What the hell had she thought?

He's going to kill you, drooled the Hag.

Ignoring that remark, Rosie returned to the sitting area with two cold beers. She handed one to the man and sat on the sofa too. They both popped the cans.

"Hello," Rosie said. To herself she thought, *Will you ravage me like Errol Flynn? Please?*

"Hello," he said and took a long drink. He looked right at home. Completely relaxed.

"My name's Rosie, and I'm here just for a few days." It sounded dumb, even to herself. *No, how can I think that? Errol Flynn? I am not that old! I will behave...like Mother taught me, knees together.*

"Rosie? Like in the *African Queen*? I like that. I'm Steve." He was sitting in the middle of the sofa with his arms spread across the back. His voice went up and down like the roll of a wave with a country twang. His feet were spread apart on the carpet, and his hard-earned stomach made a comfortable mound in front. "Thanks for the beer the other night. You saved my sanity. I didn't plan on stopping here. Wanted to go on north to Mount Pleasant but developed some problems, so I pulled in here at the last minute. Didn't know it would be all closed up. Should've radioed before stopping."

"Oh my," said Rosie, as stiff as he was relaxed. She noticed his skin was wrinkled and leathery from wind and sun. He had very blue eyes. His hair was a mixture of blond, gray, bleached blond, and a little dark brown. She wondered whether he had sustained any lasting injuries from the zipper accident that night. *Knees together.*

Suddenly she realized it was quiet, and she jerked her eyes away from his crotch, where they had wandered after that last thought, to find his eyes on her face and a slow smile on his lips.

"Your dog is real cute," she blurted out too quickly, her face turning pink.

"Yes, it is. And so is Jigger."

Rosie was stunned into silence. Then she began to giggle, then laugh out loud.

"You want to see?" he offered with the same slow smile.

"No!" she quickly said. Then she added, "Not tonight." Knees not so tightly together.

Conversation flowed easily after that exchange.

He told her that he had retired from the navy after a couple of decades on submarines. His marriage had ended three years ago. His wife got the house and car, and he got the boat and the dog. The two children were grown and doing well on their own. His needs were few. The navy retirement check covered those. When he needed more, he would put into a port and work for a few weeks and then shove off again. He had friends up and down the Eastern Seaboard. Life was good. No ties. After the stress of being encased in an iron lung underwater for months at a time and dealing with a restless wife and children he hardly knew, Steve was remaining restraint-free.

"At present," he said, "I was on my way south when I got a call from a buddy in Mount Pleasant. He asked me to stop by to give him a hand with some engine repair. I was already in Beaufort, so I had to backtrack. Here I am. A few miles short and with engine trouble of my own."

Rosie told him her story. The abbreviated version. She told him she had been married, was recently widowed, had three great adult daughters, and lived on her own. Many facts were left out, which she assumed was true of his story also. She did not include why she was here alone at this time of year. Why burden each other with the pain, defeats, humiliations, and other shit that life had dealt along the years?

Suddenly Hades leapt onto the sofa and dashed across Steve's lap with Jigger at her heels.

"Jigger!" Steve yelled. "Be still." Jigger stopped, gave him a sharp look and a wag, and took off again. The two dogs rolled over each other and snapped at each other's tails and then sat and looked at their humans with expectant faces.

Out. Out. Quick.

Rosie nodded to Hades and reached for the leash, which she fixed around the happy dog's little neck.

Steve stood and stretched out his arm to see the time. "Wow, it's midnight. Jigger, let's go." Rosie did a double take at his watch—she hadn't been up that late since Roy died. What fun!

Steve put his jacket back on and slid his feet into the sandals. "I enjoyed this. Why don't you walk me back to my boat? It's not far."

Rosie pulled the glass door shut, and she and Hades followed the big man with the tiny dog down the dock. Hades was amazed that Jigger did not have a leash on, but being a well-mannered dog, she said nothing. Little clouds of steam flowed from the faces of the group as they stomped and tapped down the wooden planks.

Steve's home was a stout white boat with brown trim. It rocked gently in the dark water. The darkness made it seem otherworldly. Steve stepped up over the rail and into the stern of the boat. He reached down and offered Rosie his hand.

"Come on aboard, Rosie, and see my little castle."

No way. Hades beat a fast, drunken walk back up the planks until the leash pulled Rosie's arm out from her side. Jigger yapped and wagged at the coward.

"Not tonight, I guess." Rosie smiled.

"Thanks for the evening." Steve gave that slow smile that made Rosie feel warm all over. His voice rose and fell lazily. "I'm expecting some friends to sail in the day after Christmas to lend a hand with my engine so I can go lend a hand to my bud in Mount Pleasant. Pop by for a drink about sunset." He was a couple of heads higher than Rosie, and he stood with one foot on the boat's rail and one hand on a stay. His stance and that beard against the starry night gave him a very rakish look. He looked almost like Errol Flynn—a well-stomached Flynn—swashbuckling across the deck of a man-of-war.

Oh shit, thought Rosie, and then she recovered enough to say, "Maybe. I enjoyed it too." She turned and let the

Chihuahua lead her back to the strip of grass and then into the warm condo.

She was shaking by the time she sat back down in her chair. She did not know if it was the cold or the desire for a man that racked her body. Hades sat in her lap and looked at her.

I saved you from a fate worse than death.

"What are you, my mother?" Rosie asked.

No, just a damn cold dog. With that Hades disappeared into her little house and settled on her heating pad.

Rosie closed up the front room. She took a long, hot bubble bath by candlelight. While she relaxed in the steamy water, she let her mind wander over the evening. Interesting. Fun. Scary. Rosie slipped into bed and called for Hades. The fact that Hades could leap into a bed several times her height always amazed Rosie. "How do you do that?" she asked sleepily.

The very warm little dog snuggled up to Rosie's ample tummy. *I love you.*

"I love you too."

* * *

Christmas Day began cold, bright, and quiet. Rosie fixed a cup of coffee and opened the few presents she had brought down with her. The youngest daughter, Izzy, had mailed several packages for her mom to have under the tree: a desk waterfall and a tiny wind chime for the inside of a room. Rosie's brother and sister-in-law had also sent a small gift: very sweet-smelling lavender sachets. The other girls would see her soon.

After a quick walk with Hades, who was surprisingly closemouthed, Rosie dressed for the visit to the old folks' home. She made sure Hades was comfortable in front of the glass doors with plenty of toys and food to eat. She took a quick glance at the white boat with brown trim, but she did not have the time to give the crew much thought.

Once in the car with cruise control set, Rosie gave in to daydreaming. Who was Steve? Should she just go with the flow? Forget him? She reached down to the radio to set the dial on 102.5, because the oldies made her feel young and carefree. Damn, even the oldies station had Christmas music. The Taurus moved smoothly up the interstate, passing little traffic.

I will stop by for that drink. Meet new people. Why not? Her head moved to a jazzy "Jingle Bells" flowing through the car. She was determined not to think of the terrifying scene that awaited her at the home.

Rosie dreaded seeing the old people at the home. The eyes in those wrinkled faces reminded Rosie of the poor dogs at the adoption affair where she had gotten Hades. *Please, God, keep Gee in a calm mood. And keep my mouth hushed!*

Maybe we will even go sailing. Scenes of Steve without his clothes were taking shape in her very imaginative mind. Gee would scream and fuss at her if she could see the pictures in Rosie's mind. Gee did not believe in sex of any kind before marriage, even for a woman at the age of 50. Once Gee had pulled a paper bag over her own head when Rosie had tried to ask about sex. No, Gee would not approve of these thoughts.

Give it up, dummy. You, cavorting nude with a stranger. Give me a break. He will die of shock when he gets a sight of that tub you use for a body. The Hag was in good form!

Rosie quickly fumbled with the radio to find a loud, fast song that could drown out the Hag. The car swayed because of her distraction. She jerked the wheel back on track and relocated 102.5. "Silver Bells" could not compete with the Hag. Rosie sang along with the music, trying to lose the evil whisper.

The Hag would not give up. *Oh, I can see it now...here a scar, there a scar,* the nasty voice hummed.

Rosie's back slumped a little, and she quit singing as she thought about the marks age, giving birth, the stress of living with Roy, and sloth had put on her once-slim form.

Rosie, Rosie, round as posies, cannot touch her toesies.

Rosie, Rosie sits on her tushy, cannot see her pussy.

Rosie, Rosie has a hard time puttin' on panty hosies.

The Hag also had that black, wicked humor. But she used it to draw blood and kill. Rosie had heard all this before, but it twisted her heart just the same. At this rate she would be a weeping blob of quivering, wrinkled flesh by the time she arrived at the home.

It was Christmas, and Rosie was determined to enter the home with at least a pretense of good cheer. The Supremes began to fill the car with "baby love, my baby love," and that was a lift for a few seconds. Rosie moved to the center lane, increasing her speed, and she pushed in cruise control again.

The Hag began all over: *You know she did not love you as much as she loved your brother and sister. You weren't as pretty or smart and didn't bring home the attractive friends. She didn't keep house for you long enough for you to get out of school. You have been helping to care for her for decades, while she didn't even do it for you for eighteen years. Stupid!*

Rosie could not hear the radio anymore. The Hag was a tangible presence in the car. Rosie sat with no expression on her face, feeling dead, driving by rote. The Hag was in control. The Hag bit away hunks of her heart and ate them right in front of her. By the time the car pulled into the long driveway to the home, the Hag was starting in all over about why she was alone for Christmas, alone all the time. Rosie stopped the car near the front entrance. Her hands gripped the steering wheel until her knuckles were white. Her head bent down and rested on the wheel between the two pale, liver-spotted fists.

Why do you fight so hard? Just give it up!

I don't know. Why? she asked herself.

Her sister would arrive any minute, and their mother was waiting for them, waiting in that living hell. That place of the living dead. Rosie bit back tears, took several cleansing breaths, and got out of the car to load up the packages she had brought for her mother. She straightened her black pants and the red jacket, made sure the scarf was even, and headed into the home, determined to act happy.

The home was a good place. It was pretty and clean. The staff and the clients always spoke to visitors in a friendly way. The entrance hall held a little Christmas tree and a huge live flower arrangement. In the large sitting room, a small old lady was banging out Christmas songs while a few quavering voices hummed in the background. Wonderful dining room smells wafted through the air around the huge dining hall. It really was a happy, busy place. It gave these old people care and community.

In spite of its good points, Rosie could never forget it was a place people came to die, the end of the road, the point of no return, the place the chariot swung low.

Rosie walked back to the clinic where her mother stayed. She could feel the Hag gathering and storing wonderful rockets and missiles to hurl at her later. The clinic was the end of the road, the last stop, a way station for the sweet chariot. Nurses and aides greeted Rosie with "Merry Christmas" and "Happy New Year." The hall was brightly decorated with plastic green swags of cedar that hung over each doorway where some poor old body sat propped up in a bed or chair. To reach her mother's room, Rosie walked through the general sitting area by the main nurses' station. The nurse behind the high workstation did not even look up as an old woman in a wheelchair held her teeth out and requested over and over for someone to please wash them. Under a handwritten sign that stated the date, the season, and the location, an elderly man sat belted in his chair and looked out with dull, blank eyes. Several other remnants of once active and productive people were placed around the bright area. Rosie found this almost the worst part of visiting her mother.

Her mother shared a room. The roommates had changed over the years as one after the other died. The home always put an old lady who could not talk and who could hear very little in the room with her mother because her mother did not make a very gentle, cooperative roomie. Her mother was bedridden most of the time, but with help, she could dress and get around in a wheelchair. This morning she was up and dressed in the green dress with white dots that she had worn for years. Her hair was fixed, her makeup was on, and she had a shiny pin at the neck of her dress. Ada was a fine-boned woman who had never put on weight or lost her figure. Wrinkles and liver spots had done their work to mar a once extremely beautiful face, but her eyes were still sharp, as was her tongue. Shaky hands were holding a compact up so Ada could powder her nose and at the same time shock herself by once again seeing that, yes, she did look like an old lady.

"Merry Christmas, Mama," Rosie sang as she entered the room.

"Merry Christmas yourself," Ada replied and held up her cheek for a kiss.

Rosie bent over and pecked the withered cheek. She loved the way her mother smelled. Not even the horrors of aging in a place that often reeked of Pine-Sol could hide the sweet aromas of childhood that the old lady exuded. Rosie put her packages and bags on the floor.

"Is Chick here?"

"Who?"

"Chick, your other daughter," Rosie replied. "My sister."

"I don't know if she was here today or if that was yesterday."

"You look very pretty, Mama."

"How can you say that? Have you looked at me?" Ada asked as she held up a shaky, blue-veined hand.

Rosie never knew how to answer this, so she picked up a comb from the bedside table and began to stroke through the thin gray hair. "Yes, I have looked at you, you old lady, and you look damn good." This made her mother chuckle. Her rare laughter gave Rosie hope for a good day after all.

Over the noises of the hall, Rosie could hear the approach of her sister. She walked with firm, quick clacks of her heels on the hard floor, not the soft squeak of the staff in their comfortable rubber-soled shoes. Chick swept into the small room with an armful of packages wrapped in bright reds and greens and tied with huge gold bows. Being an artist with flair, she dressed the same way. Her neat body was encased in a form-fitting dark green dress, a gold beret tilted to one side on her small head, and thrown around her slim shoulders was a bright red woolen wrap with big tassels that swung with her steps.

"Merry Christmas," Chick chirped, and she began to unload. "Mother, you look great. Did you eat breakfast? Rosie, how are you, dear?" Without waiting for answers, she settled on the side of the bed and began to spread packages around. Chick had her own personal Hag but always seemed in better control of it than Rosie ever felt.

The small area in the clinic room became a happy Christmas morning for a short time. Pain, old age, and hurt feelings were forgotten while the old face lit up with joy as Ada unwrapped the pile of gifts collected at the foot of the bed. Chick and Rosie took turns explaining who had sent the packages. "This is from your granddaughter. Your son's child, Carrie."

Ada interrupted, "I thought Carrie was your son."

"No, my son is Sam," Chick said. She and Rosie doubled over with giggles. "Carrie is William's daughter, and Jane is her little daughter."

"Her little daughter? I thought Jane lived with Rosie and went to Ethiopia."

Rosie replied, "I don't have a Jane. But this gift is from little Jane. And it was my daughter, Izzy, who went to Ethiopia."

"Why did she go to China? Who made her go? What is this?" Ada asked as she held a picture in a silver frame upside down and stared at it. She had forgotten China for the time being.

When all the packages had been opened, Ada demanded her liquor. Nothing cheered the old lady more than a shot of bourbon—and not just any bourbon. It had to be 90 proof and straight up.

Chick quickly tried to divert the bourbon question by looking at her watch and announcing it was time for dinner.

"But I need my drink to help me eat," Ada firmly said. Ada had not eaten more than five spoonfuls of food for a meal in thirty years but always swore the liquor gave her a powerful appetite. She grasped the arms of her wheelchair with gnarled fingers, hunched her bony shoulders up to her elongated ears, and snarled through thin lips, "I want my drink." She got her drink.

"The drink" had been a bone of contention for years. Rosie felt what the hell, let the old lady have a little pleasure. Chick always gave her California-influenced opinion. The drink was not good for her and might interact with her meds. Alcohol was just not good for the body, Chick argued. Rosie always countered with "Is she going to run a race or have a baby, for God's sake?" But it was true that Ada became even more snappy and mean when she imbibed. Ada's doctor settled the issue, but not the disagreement, by stopping all meds and giving the sweet old dear three snorts of bourbon a day.

Rosie pushed the wheelchair while Chick helped Ada choose her meal as they moved slowly through the food line. Finally they set their plates on a round table in the midst of the old bodies that had nowhere to go for the holidays. Many had outlived their children or had simply been forgotten. The large dining room had been decorated with the best plastic money could buy.

Rosie tucked right into her dish of turkey and dressing. Chick daintily pushed some food around her plate while eyeing it with a California-trained mind and frowned in disgust. Ada, who loudly claimed all the food was horrid, just stared around as if she had not eaten in that room for the past twenty years.

"Just look at that man with all that facial hair. I cannot believe men are so weak as to do that!" Ada whispered at the top of her lungs. She pointed a bony, bent finger toward a middle-aged man seated with an ancient old gent who was using both palsied hands to get a dripping fork to his gaping mouth.

"Mother, he can hear you," Rosie squeaked in embarrassment as the bearded man glanced in their direction.

But Ada would not give it up. "I think he must be a homosexual. A real man would not look like that!" Her voice rose. "What you children have to put up with today in this world. I did not know what men did with each other until I was married and your father told me."

There was silence at the table.

"Is that woman colored? She is so dark." Ada sneered. "They are taking over the world. Everywhere you look there is a foreigner."

Chick covered her mother's thin hand with her own thin hand, gritted her teeth, and very softly said, "Shut up, old woman." Ada frowned at this rude remark.

"Peggy, I mean Star, William, *Rosie*," Ada finally got out after naming far-flung family members, voice rising. "What did we watch the last time you were here? You know, the one with the little black babies in the trees? We laughed and laughed."

Oh God, thought Rosie, *how can she remember that now?* A month ago they had spent the afternoon in her mother's room with Ada nodding off now and then and Rosie reading the *Post and Courier* Sunday edition newspaper while the TV yammered in the background. It was a challenge to make sure nothing like scantily clad gyrating bodies or Democrats filled the screen. Ada was prone to long, angry lectures on the ruin of the world if she saw anything less than twenty-five years old on TV. Rosie had settled on Animal Planet, because what could animals do as long as they were not doing "it"?

"What was it? Tell Chick about it," Ada prompted again.

With her face almost in the rice and gravy, Rosie muttered, "It was Animal Planet, and they were monkeys, not people, Mother."

"Looked like little colored babies to me. What is wrong with me saying what I want to?" Ada snapped. The bourbon had kicked in.

Ada ate all of one half ounce of food, Chick ate a little salad, and Rosie polished off a ton of Christmas turkey, rice, dressing, something cheesy, greens, and then a big slice of cake. Rosie loved Christmas food, and packing it in in front of these two scarecrows made it even better. They all ate in silence, heads lowered as if they were trying to disappear.

Oh goody, I cannot wait for the wee dark hours! The Hag thought, rubbing her nasty hands together in glee.

The rest of the afternoon passed in a false "Be nice" and "Aren't we having fun?" atmosphere until 2:30 p.m., when the sisters kissed their mother on her old, sagging cheeks and slumped to their respective cars to depart. Christmas had always been a time of great expectations and even greater stress. Small unspoken concerns and doubts gnawed away at hearts all the holiday season.

By Christmas afternoon nerves were raw, exposed, and easily jangled. It was the tradition, and, by damn, you had better be a quivering mass of defeat and disappointment by Christmas evening or you were not a true member of *this* family! Each sister drove with a heavy foot on the gas, but neither was able to outrun her personal Hag, who settled in with a smirk and a promise of a nasty night to come.

* * *

"Come out to the boat tonight," Steve said the next day as he balanced a bag of groceries with one arm and carried his dog with the other. Cold wind whipped through the old trees, but the sky was clear and bright. Rosie had just pulled up to the gate at the condos to find Steve walking from the little ship's store across the almost-empty parking lot. Hades sat curled behind Rosie's neck and snapped and snarled at her little doggy friend, who yapped something nasty back.

"Be there by seven, very informal, dress warm, and bring Hades. Bye." And he made his way down the footpath around the gate and through the large bushes to the dock. Rosie stared at the still-closed gate and then got out and punched in the code.

Inside Rosie flopped on the bed and wondered whether she would go to supper at the dock. She had not recovered from the horrible Christmas the day before. Shopping this morning had helped a little. A sleeping pill last night had helped a lot. She felt numb.

Go ahead, chubs, put on a heavy sweater. Dress warm. Hips ahoy!

She bunched the pillow up around her head to shut the voice out. When had the voice started? How had it gotten so loud and demanding? Childhood?

Ah, childhood! A time of loving family members who cheered your triumphs, kissed away your hurts, and laughed at your silly jokes. A time of cheerful meals in front of a glowing fireplace. A time of going to church hand in hand with mothers and fathers. *Bullshit!* The movie in Rosie's head flipped back through the years. Rosie was a captive audience, unable to stop the film, unable to turn off the sound. There were just jerky vignettes that appeared out of sequence, dancing in her head.

One that seemed to repeat a lot was the time when Rosie found out where potluck dinners came from. Once or twice a year, the pastor at church announced there would be a picnic after the service. Rosie loved this: so much good food set up on tables under the pecan trees behind the church. One beautiful day when the whole church was out there, a very Christian lady looked at Rosie and, with a mean smile, asked which dish her mother had fixed. Rosie was stunned. Mothers fixed all this food? Mothers made this wonderful event? Rosie had never wondered where the dishes had come from. Now she threw her paper plate in the trash and ran home. Rosie walked herself around the corner from her house to the church, but she walked alone, even on Mother's Day. Ada never went to church, PTA meetings, football games, movies—anywhere with Rosie. After that crushing humiliation at the picnic, Rosie never went back to church, and nobody from the church ever came looking for her.

Another incident that was burned into her memory was the time she had seen her father horsewhip her brother. Her brother was a teenager and really had done nothing to rile the old man but was rewarded nonetheless with a beating with a real horse whip. Oh yes, family life was a nightmare that Rosie had tried and tried to whitewash, but the memories always stayed dirty and dark. There were a couple of memories she could now laugh at, like when her sister had tied her to a tree and painted her yellow just because there was some leftover paint in the garage. Oh hell, family was just too good! At last Rosie slept, deeply.

As the sun set over the marsh in great red splendor, Rosie awoke feeling as if she were emerging from a bed of quicksand surrounded by a thick fog. She rubbed her face to wipe away the confusion. The invitation to the boat snapped into her mind. She would go and have a good time and everything else be damned!

Take a quick shower. Pull on something warm. Don't look in the mirror more than necessary to quickly do the eyes and lips. Don't look below the neck. Snap on the leash. Move so quickly the mind cannot interfere. Once she had accomplished these tasks, Rosie locked the sliding door and headed down the wooden walk to the boat, with Hades's little feet clicking on the boards.

She stopped short at the bow of the boat. The whole vessel was aglow with light. Christmas music bounced from the cabin. What in the hell was she doing here?

We are going to have fun, old lady. I'm cold, cold. The little dog pulled at the leash as she sniffed the warm air rising from the boat. *Get with it.*

"What's got you so brave all of a sudden?"

Rosie heaved her weight over the rail and onto the boat before she lost her nerve. She was not sure where to step or what to do with the dog. "Hello?" she weakly called. "Hello?" she called again, a little stronger.

Bark, bark, shouted the more confident Hades.

"Welcome aboard," came a warm male voice. "Come on down the ladder."

Rosie stood with the dog clutched to her breast and stared down the open hatch into a pool of yellow light and a broad, smiling face. She gingerly stepped onto the first rung of the ladder, swung her backside around, and began to lower herself awkwardly into the cabin. Slowly she backed down the steps, not knowing that Steve had moved so close that she essentially sat on his upturned face. A scream ripped from her throat as his teeth closed with a quick nip on a mouthful of her rump. She lost her footing and floundered in midair, with the dog yapping at the top of her tiny lungs. All this caused her to fall heavily, fanny first, into Steve's open arms. They toppled over backward, landing with a solid thump that made the boat quiver. Jigger joined the fray, and both dogs screeched and began to lick each other and both humans. Legs, hair, fur, arms, tongues, tails, and voices tangled, screamed, laughed, and licked until, breathless, they all four sat staring at each other and pulling themselves together.

"Hell, woman, you know how to make an entrance," Steve said, wiping tears and fur from his eyes. "What will you have to drink?"

"A bourbon and Diet Coke would be nice."

Rosie studied the cabin. It was small, efficient, homey, and very warm. Warm like when you were a little child and bundled in front of an open fire, growing sleepy as the cold lost its grip on your body. She sat on the edge of a bunk filled with soft pillows and blankets. There were books and a lot of boat stuff scattered about. She liked it. She felt at home. The dogs had disappeared somewhere up in the V-berth cabin. She could hear small doggy sounds, but her attention was drawn back to the man opening and closing small cabinet doors as he mixed two drinks in fine crystal glasses. His agility in the cramped space amazed her.

"Cheers." He handed her the drink and stood right in front of her. Right in front of her face. Right smack in front of her face. If she stuck her tongue out, it would touch his belt buckle. So she did not do that. She took the drink and downed a good portion of it.

"Thanks, I needed that." What else do you say to a belly button under a flannel shirt and above a belt buckle? She had no idea.

He gave the top of her head a pat and flopped down on the opposite bunk. He ran a hand over his hair and beard for a quick brush up. There was quiet for a moment.

"I like your boat," she said.

"Thanks."

They both sipped their drinks. His bright blue eyes twinkled.

"Hungry?" he asked.

"I don't know."

"Good, because we will eat later when the others get here."

"The others?" She had forgotten Steve had said his friends were coming. This made Rosie a little more nervous and a little disappointed.

"Remember I told you that I was headed to help a friend repair his engine? But I ended up here? Well, he and a date are driving down for dinner. It's only an hour by car but half a day by boat. I think you will find him interesting."

He reached up and flicked a switch to change the music to something a little softer and easier to talk over. Classic rock, easy-listening music, gently took over. He rose from the bunk, stepped over to the little galley and began to pull things from the cabinets.

"Can I help?"

"Sure." He tossed her a head of lettuce. "Salad."

They talked and fixed dinner. He handed her this and that. She found what she needed and produced an interesting dish. With both of them in the tight galley, there was a lot of squeezing past each other and reaching over one another. She found it strange, but he was so relaxed and at ease that she quickly felt right at home. He soon had things sizzling on the stove.

"Ahoy there!" a loud, deep voice shouted.

Steve stepped up the ladder and stuck his head out the hatch. "Come aboard."

The boat rocked gently as heavy feet boarded. Rosie moved back from the galley and ladder and settled on a bunk. Steve went back to the stove, stirring the wonderful-smelling pan of food.

A large bare foot felt its way onto the second rung of the ladder. It was the strangest foot Rosie had ever seen. It was blue and red with slashes of scar tissue running over it. The foot was attached to a calf, then a knee, then a thigh, which all had the appearance of having been assembled by a blind person from pieces of a puzzle. Rosie could not help but stare. Another foot and leg followed. A naked behind filled the hatch. The behind was withered by age but had the same drunken puzzle pattern as the legs. Hanging between the thighs were two of the biggest balls Rosie had ever imagined. Her hand flew to her face to cover her eyes.

"What's for supper?" the deep voice asked. Several healthy back slaps followed as the two men greeted each other.

"Where is your date?" Steve asked.

"No date. Who is this?"

Never had Rosie ever imagined such a scene. Before her stood a completely naked man resembling an aged Viking whose skin had been designed by an unsighted but very detail-oriented quilter. He had broad shoulders; a flat, rippling abdomen; a generous, smiling mouth in a brush of beard; bright blue eyes under a shag of bleached hair; pieces of ears; and gnarled hands. This had once been a mighty good-looking man. The skin looked as if irregular pieces of cloth had been dyed strange flesh colors and then sewn back together. You could see where the needle had gone in and out. Rosie's attention was drawn back down the beautiful, strange torso to settle on the small ruin of what once must have been the proud tower of much pleasure.

"Rosie, Charlie. Charlie, Rosie. I'm fixing steaks and salad for dinner. Want a drink?"

"Yes," said Rosie, and she held out her half-empty glass.

Both men rumbled a laugh deep in their throats, and Charlie settled on the bunk by Rosie. Steve turned to prepare drinks. Rosie didn't know what to think. She tried to make herself small in her place on the bunk. That sure did not work. Should she look away? Stare? She had never dreamed of such a scene.

"My God, what happened to you?" Rosie blurted out.

Charlie got up to lean against the mast that ran up through the middle of the cabin. He crossed his arms over his chest and let his eyes focus on something long ago and far away. "It was...it was a terrible thing that happened to me. I was sailing up the Amazon with a crew of friends in search of a lost tribe someone told us about." He looked down at Rosie, who was entranced with every word. "We dropped anchor, thinking we would be safe because there was nothing but jungle around. It was so quiet and dark. We never heard the dugout slip up next to our boat. They swarmed over the edge and grabbed us. They were small and dark with chopped-off black hair. It took four of them to tie me up."

"My God," Rosie whispered, downing a huge mouthful of alcohol.

"They threw us overboard and hauled us to shore. There was a big fire. Drums. There must've been thousands of them."

"What did you do?"

"I was scared. I felt like Gulliver with all these little pissant men swarming all over me. I could've picked up three in one arm." He raised one arm over his head, which was not high in the close cabin, as he leaned closer into her with his eyes flashing sparks through what was left of his burned-off bushy eyebrows.

"For Gawd's sake! Give me a break," Steve hooted. "The old man got drunk and burned his ass up in his own boat. He looks like that because he was supposed to die. The doctors just slapped what skin was left over burned spots. They didn't think he would make it, so they didn't pay attention to what the finished product would look like."

"Good story, though, wasn't it?" Charlie asked as he sat back down. This time he was really close to Rosie. He shifted his weight so one hip stuck out. "See that spot?" He pointed to his hip. "Well, this tattoo used to be there." Now he pointed to a blurry green cat that was stretched across his left arm right above the wrist.

Rosie was speechless. A very naked madman and a round-bellied cook getting more soused by the minute were more than she could take in right then. Rosie had seen Roy nude, of course. But she had never been in a social situation where people stood around drinking and talking and were nude. Rosie could hear her mother's sneering voice tell her how evil this was, how Hollywood had caused this tear in morality, and on and on. He did not *look* naked. With the burn scars, the few tattoos, and his easy stance, he just looked undressed, Rosie reasoned. Yes, undressed. So Rosie began to relax and decided to go with the flow of these strange, friendly boatpeople.

"Well," she said in a very whispery voice, "well, well, well. I never."

"Well, I'll be happy to be sure you do before you leave the boat," answered the very naked man, and he placed a long arm over her shoulders.

Rosie leapt up and moved to the other bunk. At her movement Hades, with Jigger on her heels, bounced into the cabin and onto Rosie's lap. From that position the tiny black dog began to lecture the very naked man on the way to treat her mother. She spoke at the top of her lungs. Jigger repeated every other word.

"Be quiet, you boat rats!" Steve shouted over the noise. "Rosie, here are the plates. Put some of that salad you made on them, and I will slap the meat on and we can eat."

The evening continued until the wee hours of the morning. The men told stories—each trying to outdo the other and both laughing until tears ran down their cheeks. Rosie said little but ached from laughing at the raunchy humor of the men. The dogs fell asleep after licking steak juice from the plates. No one even cared that the plates were still on the table and that the agile dogs had jumped up there when they knew the people were beyond being concerned about the dishes. The male voices, the warm little dog bodies, and a third bottle of red wine created a perfect world.

Eventually, Charlie dozed off, and the cabin grew quiet.

"I better go," said Rosie.

"You could stay," Steve said.

Rosie looked at him and thought of all the long nights she had spent alone. He looked good. She was on the verge of saying, "Yes, I'll stay," when Hades sprang awake and jumped up into her face with an intent stare and nervous wags of her tail.

Rosie looked into Hades's face and said, "You're right." She rose from the bunk, removed a blanket from the shelf above, and spread it over the sleeping, very naked man. "I'm not able to stay. Maybe another night."

"I'm leaving tomorrow. Charlie brought the part I needed, and we'll fix the engine in the morning. I'll leave with the tide after lunch." He put his arms around her. "Stay with me."

"No," she said quickly, and she gently pushed him away. "My body shouts 'yes,' but the rest of me is not strong enough. Another time? I'm down here a lot."

"I can't stay. I promised friends I would help them. Remember I told you? And I am already a couple of days behind." He pulled her close again and kissed her. "But," he added as he slid his mouth across her cheek to her ear, "I go up and down this way often." He pushed his hips up and down her thigh for emphasis and, smiling, said, "You're good company. Another time for sure."

"I'll look for your boat." She freed herself and turned back to the ladder leading up to the stern deck.

"Give me your phone number, and I'll call you when I'm headed this way. Will you do that?" He had moved close to her again and placed his big hands on her face to lift her mouth to his. "Will you?"

"My phone number?" She had no idea what her phone number was. Blood was racing through her head, and her knees were growing weak. She managed to turn her head and saw a pencil by a notepad. Shakily she scribbled down a number. "I think that's it," she gasped, and she bent down to scoop up Hades.

He slowly and firmly ran his warm hand over her behind, giving her crotch a strong nudge.

"Oh my God. Good night," she barely whispered, and she somehow got her weak body and the little dog up to the cold, fresh air and onto the dock. "Oh—I had a good time," she called to him as she fled back to the condo.

As she lay in bed with the covers drawn up to her chin, she told Hades, "Thank you, you wonderful dog. It would have been a bad mistake. Fun. A lot of fun. But a mistake. Next time we will be ready for a good fling. We will work on my mind. Right?" she asked the tiny head that poked out from the covers right between her breasts.

Right. Right. You did right. Humans should be like dogs. Be quick and then forget it. Forget it.

Rosie laughed to herself. *Would that I could, would that I could. Be quick and then forget it*, Rosie thought. *But my heart gets in the way*. She turned onto her side and drifted off, wondering whether the evening had been real or a dream. Who were those strange men?

* * *

It was early afternoon when Rosie swam up from a deep sleep where she and Steve had enjoyed hours of stimulating "fun." Hades had been up for hours, watching the dock through the glass doors. Rosie staggered into the kitchen to warm some coffee. She caught a glimpse of her reflection in the oven door—swollen, plump, red face; hair going this way and that; faded night T-shirt. Yuck!

With a steaming mug of instant coffee in hand, Rosie slumped onto the sofa and gazed at the dock. Was it all a dream? Was it part dream? She sipped the coffee. It was hard for her mind to sort out the truth from the remains of the exciting dreams. Slowly her mind cleared and then snapped to attention when she remembered Steve was leaving today. She jumped to the glass doors to spot his boat at the dock.

There were no boats at the dock. There were just dark water, brown marsh, and cold blue sky.

"He's gone. Gone."

But Jigger told me they would be back in the spring. I like Jigger.

Rosie stood at the door a long time, staring at the little harbor. *Why didn't I just jump into bed with him?* she asked herself. To her surprise the Hag did not make a nasty remark. She searched her mind, looking for a trap. The Hag was good at mind games. No Hag. The ending of *The Great Gatsby* floated into her head: we are all in a boat going against the tide toward the future, but we are pushed back to the shores of memory—or something like that.

She'll be back. She is scared of test—test—testosterone. Hades stammered over the big word.

Rosie kept herself busy making Christmas phone calls to everyone she could think of. Then she cleaned the condo until it looked better than brand new.

Why did it always take more space to pack up for the return home than it had taken to begin with? Rosie stuffed sweaters and gifts into bags. After an hour of hauling stuff to the car and checking the condo to be sure all was shut down, Rosie and Hades sat in the car, waiting for the tall gate to swing open and allow them to leave.

Good time. I had a good time. I like Jigger.

Me too, little one, Rosie thought in return.

Hades assumed her driving position by inserting herself between the top of the seat and Rosie's neck. Rosie didn't mind at all because the day was bitterly cold, and the warmth from the furry body felt good.

Home? Home?

"No, little one, not yet. We're going downtown to see Chick, and you can look for the cat. We'll spend the night with her."

Hades snorted in disgust and snuggled down on her neck.

There was not much traffic on Bohicket Road, as it was still so soon after Christmas. Rosie enjoyed driving under the trees with their tendrils of Spanish moss dancing in the wind. She turned onto Maybank Highway, where traffic was a little heavier. It was the first time since she had walked away from the empty dock that she allowed herself to think about last night on the boat.

Her mind went over both of the evenings with Steve. She played every little sentence over and over in her mind. It made her smile as she drove. Women were so different from men. Steve would be occupied with some greasy boat engine, never giving Rosie a thought. He wasn't crass, but he was a man. He might think of her when someone asked what he had been doing. But he was surely not rehashing every scene with her. Being a footloose and fancy-free sailor of the world, he had had thousands of such nights, so the time with her would not seem as important or out of the ordinary. It had been to Rosie.

That had been the first time in years she had felt a man's eyes on her, and it had made her feel good. She felt strong and attractive.

She was not a child or even a "young thing." She was over fifty, overweight, and over having overblown expectations. It was not love. He would not sail up in a white boat to whisk her away to happily ever after. She was glad she knew that and could accept it. Yeah, dream on, she would enjoy thinking about it and could hope he would return one day. Sometimes being mature had its advantages. If she had been twenty-five or thirty, she—oh hell—she would have screwed his balls off! Maybe next time she would. Yes, she would.

Thinking too much. You are thinking too much, Hades worried.

I know. Back to the Zen. Enjoy the present. Be here, now, she told herself. As she drove over the Ashley River Bridge and into the city, she could see a fiery red winter sunset in the rearview mirror.

Hades stuck her nose up to the top of window Rosie had cracked a tiny bit and loudly sniffed the air. *What is that smell? That horrible smell?*

"That, little one, is the smell of the Low Country, the smell of history, the smell of our bloodline."

Maybe yours, Hades muttered, letting loose a big sneeze and sticking her cold nose against Rosie's neck.

"You are right again," Rosie chuckled. "It is the harbor mud at really low tide spiced with sewage. But you already guessed that! Pluff mud."

Rosie threaded her way through the one-way streets that led down the peninsula. It was fun to drive very slowly so she could see into the well-lighted windows of the huge antebellum homes and check out the decorations. It was a lot cheaper than waiting for the spring house tours. The problem was that she could see only the upper halves of the rooms, but that was still enough to glimpse the color schemes and the tops of the huge antique pieces of furniture.

On a whim she decided to drive around the Battery. It was not deep dark yet, so she could make out the shapes of a dozen sailboats bobbing across the harbor. The little boats looked like toys with tiny lights. It was hard to imagine people moving around in the small dots on the gently rolling waters where the Ashley River and the Cooper River met the Atlantic Ocean. But she knew each little boat was alive with some activity important only to the people inside. Were Steve and Jigger in one of those, or had they already rounded the Battery and disappeared up the Intracoastal Waterway?

"Hell! We are going to be late!" Rosie announced, and she made a quick turn onto South Battery and headed for her sister's. As she went up Meeting Street, she noticed a white Jaguar parked on the street. She rarely thought of Roy and that night, but the white car flooded her mind with bitter memories of her wasted years of life with a drunk.

No, you don't. Rosie could hear Hades in her ear. *No, you don't go down that dark path tonight.* Life was to be lived now, not last night, last year, or tomorrow. There were things to be done and places to go. So she went.

Valentine's Day

2015

January had been a very good month. Rosie was busy at church with altar duty again and helping with family-night suppers. She had been to see Gee a couple of times. Early on New Year's Eve they had shared a bottle of champagne. Chick had gone back somewhere out west to take an art class. William had been right: Rosie was living and working.

The school system had been very good to Rosie. She had loved teaching, but the strain of bringing up three daughters and living with a mean drunk had taken its toll. Finally, in 2012, she had to resign from the classroom because she began to throw up before leaving the house and often after lunch. She developed hives and clenched her teeth together so tightly she woke up with sore jaws. The added stress of being locked in a trailer stuffed with hormonal, horny, antsy teens had to end.

"However," said the principal, "we have an opening in working with new teachers. You could do the observing and recording—it's only a few times a month, but the pay is good. And you can sub when we run short. You will be perfect after you are trained." So Rosie got trained and began her new part time position, and she loved it.

* * *

This weekend, for Valentine's Day, Rosie had decided to go to Bohicket and just relax with Hades. It was warm enough to bundle up and walk on the beach. So they packed up and headed south. It did not take long to quickly pick up groceries and settle in for the weekend.

She pushed the swing back and forth with her bare toes as she sipped her vodka and studied the boats rocking in the dark water at the dock. Several men walked by on their way to their beloved boats. They nodded and waved to her. The air was cool, but the sky was bright. Spring was not far off. Soon everything would burst into blossom, and fragrance would fill the senses. Spring in the Low Country was better than a drink. A person could get drunk just gazing at wisteria as it trailed through the branches of the old oak trees. And the azaleas! The colors.

Both Rosie and Hades jumped when the phone rang.

"Hello," panted Rosie. She had gotten up too fast and felt a little dizzy.

"Mama, you won't believe who called you!" It was her oldest daughter. "I was at your house when he called." This child could always talk as fast as a freight train. One time when she was a little girl, she had talked to the neighbor's dog so much that the dog had hidden way back under the house. And she had never slowed down. "Mama, you won't believe it." Star had come to Mount Pleasant for a high school reunion and had stayed with Rosie for three nights of wild partying with her classmates. She was to return to Asheville the same day Rosie went to Bohicket. But being a little hungover, Star had gone back to bed after Rosie left that morning and was still there when the phone rang.

"Who, who?" Rosie managed to break in.

"I was still at your house when the phone rang."

"Who called?"

"Rob Halsey. He and his family are on their way to Orlando, and they're coming through Charleston. They want to see you. He said they would spend the night, I forgot where, but somewhere downtown, and they want to take you to dinner."

"Rob Halsey? I can't believe that." Rosie was stunned—Rob Halsey was her love from decades ago. Her love from the long-gone past. Suddenly he was here, almost right here.

"Yes, Rob Halsey," Star rushed on. "He wants you to call him at this number." She gave Rosie the number but had to repeat it because Rosie was so shocked that she kept getting the digits mixed up. "Call me back after you talk to him." And she was gone.

Rosie just looked at the phone in its cradle. Years. It had been twenty years since she had heard from Rob. It had been several years since she had even thought of him—not true, she thought of him often and envied whomever he had married. She picked up the phone but could not punch in the numbers.

Who is Rob? Who? the Chihuahua wondered to herself. *I hope this doesn't start another dark mood* ran through the little mind. *I'm not up to a fight with that nasty Hag.*

A flood of memories filled Rosie's head. And for once they were all good memories.

"I've got to do some thinking, little one. Let's go back out."

They settled back into their spots, Rosie in the swing and Hades in the sunshine nodding off again and trying to act interested as Rosie told her about Rob.

They had met in the summer between her sophomore and junior years in college. Way back in the early sixties. She had a job for the summer in Charleston, and he was doing research for his graduate degree from Harvard. He was smarter, older, richer, and much warmer (for a Yankee, that is) than she had expected from a blind date. It had been a golden summer filled with long walks on the beaches and late nights full of beer and laughter.

Charleston had not yet been discovered, so to speak, meaning it was still quiet and mysterious, filled with people who, like most of Rosie's family, had not yet become reconciled to the fact that the War of Northern Aggression had wiped out their inherited positions of wealth and power. As Rob's research was in history, they spent hours and hours walking the narrow streets and getting lost in the shadows of the past. There were hundreds of shaded spots by beautiful wrought iron garden gates that hid the entwined couple. Once they had spent a humid, sweaty night necking (and a little more) on the top of John C. Calhoun's cool marble tomb in the graveyard of St. Philip's Church. Then summer had ended, and Rob returned to the north and Rosie to her southern college campus.

They had planned to meet in Washington that November. Rob had a conference there, and Rosie told her mother she was going to visit a roommate who lived in Alexandria. The visit had been arranged since he had left at summer's close, but the friend upon whom the whole sneaky trip depended was hospitalized with a broken ankle from playing hockey. The lovers never met again, but they did write warm letters and a made few phone calls. Eventually time took its toll, and their lives went in different directions.

Rob had stayed in Rosie's heart over the decades. Should she have taken the marriage proposal she had turned down because he would have taken her up north? He had been her first real love.

Hades was fast asleep in her sunshine when Rosie ended the story with promises of more later—and there had been more. Rosie picked up the phone she had brought out to the swing and quickly hit the numbers she had written down earlier.

Immediately Rob's soft Yankee voice filled her head with "Hello." It was an older, more mature voice, but she would have known it anywhere.

"Rob? I don't believe it. Where are you? How did you find me?" God, that sounded dumb.

"You sound the same. I called your sister, and she told me how to reach you. Are you home now? Rosie?" He questioned whether she was still there, as she was still shocked by the call and hadn't answered.

"No," she said in a rush, "I'm at Bohicket on Seabrook."

"Good, we are in the car and just about to pass Florence on I-95 on our way to Disney. Thought I would swing east to show my family the old city and take you to dinner."

"My God, I don't believe this."

"Can you meet us in the lobby at the Omni at seven?"

"Yes, yes, I can." Her heart was racing.

"Good. See you then, and I am looking forward to it."

What'll I wear? Rosie ran in a tight little circle around the dog. *Hades, what to wear? What if his wife is slim and beautiful and here I am looking like me? Hades, talk to me! Oh God.*

She rushed into the condo and ran to the closet. Jeans, sweater, purple sweats. She raced through the meager clothes she had brought with her for a quiet weekend of sitting on the dock. *Black pants—thank you, God—black pants and this black top. That's good.*

Rosie stood under a strong, hot shower. Her hair was a little longer than it had been at Christmas, but it was freshly colored and would curl softly in the damp February night. As she scrubbed her ample body, she wondered at her own acceptance of this startling surprise. No Hag could be felt lurking in the corners of her mind. She just felt good and knew herself well enough not to question the good feeling so closely that it faded away to leave her spiraling down into the pit. Not tonight. It was a James Brown event—*I feel good!*

Hades was curled up on the pillow of one of the twin beds observing the dressing ritual. Suddenly she jumped up with an *I gotta go, gotta go now.* Rosie snapped on the leash, and they went for a quick walk around the parking lot so Hades could do what was necessary. As they came back into the condo, Rosie was struck by the beautiful sunset framed in the front windows. The orange sky blazed over the marsh, casting rippling reflections in the high tide. It would be dark soon.

Rosie clutched the dog to her chest and sat gingerly on the sofa. Dark. She hated driving in the dark. The road to the city was a narrow two-lane blacktop with huge oak trees on each side. There were a million ways for a car to pull into her path. It was bad enough in the day, but at night, the approaching lights seemed to take the form of floating spacecraft aimed right at her. Streetlights blossomed into gigantic disks. And just forget it if it rained.

You can do it. The bright black Chihuahua eyes bored into hers. *You can do it.*

"You are right, little one. I can and I will." Rosie's good feelings returned. She had spent long enough not doing what she wanted. Fear and dread had ruled her world. Not tonight. It was James Brown all the way!

At last she stood in front of the bathroom mirror for a last-minute check. Black pants, black top, graduated silver beads around her neck, thin silver bracelets on her wrist, and silver drop earrings. Her makeup was just right. *Oh God, please don't have a hot flash.* She liked what she saw—or rather, accepted what she saw. Tonight, with the Hag out of the way, she did not dwell on the multiple chins or the thick waist. Even the few gray hairs that had quickly shed the color job looked good. She lovingly sprayed Chanel from head to toe, which made her flee the room in a fit of coughing.

Damn, sneezed Hades. *You look tip-top, just tip-top.*

After settling the pooch and getting into the car, Rosie checked the time. It was 5:00 p.m. She had plenty of time. The darkening sky wasn't too bad. She could do this and get there with time to spare. No problem with Bohicket Road. Right at the Big Pig onto Maybank and to a complete standstill four miles later as traffic was backed up because of bridge construction. *Damn this Low Country, bridges everywhere.* Go, stop, go, stop. Now it was completely dark, and the oncoming vehicles began to take the shape of alien craft. Go, stop, go, stop. The cars slowly maneuvered through the mess of bridge construction. There was no room for a mistake. Too far to the left and that white Jaguar got you, and too far to the right and you slept with the fishes. *Oh God, how will I get back later?* Finally traffic thinned out just in time to come to a dead stop for the drawbridge over the Ashley River. *Shit.*

Sam. Sam? That was all she knew about his wife. Rosie had never liked the name Sam for a girl. Sam...Samantha...a witch. That made Rosie smile to herself. She glanced in the mirror and patted down her curly hair. Sam would have smooth hair with a touch of blond in it. She would wear dangling gold earrings and have a big glad-to-meet-you social smile pasted across her perfect face. Rob had always had high-class taste. That had scared Rosie, as she felt she was just a step or two above redneck and had no idea how to act in Ivy League settings. She thought back to the time she had visited Rob at his parents' home in New York and when dessert was announced she got excited, as dinner had been very small servings. "Dessert" was brought out... one apple and a piece of cheese for the whole table. She had laughed out loud, not good form. But then Rob had thought she was worthy of a proposal, so why had she thought so poorly of herself? Oh hell. She ran her tongue over her slightly yellowed and slightly crooked teeth to check for lipstick. That made her picture the perfect, big white teeth Sam would have. *I am as bad as the Hag—she has taught me well*, Rosie almost cried out loud.

She hit the steering wheel and could feel the beginnings of a hot flash creep over her scalp and down her neck. First the heat built up on the top of her head. Then the flush spread over her face and slowly through the rest of her body. Her glasses fogged up. Hell, even the windshield fogged a little. She could feel her makeup begin to slide with the sweat. She flapped her hand around in front of her face and opened the window. The cool air felt good and calmed her down. Ahead she could see that the bridge was beginning to close. Cars revved up in anticipation of the last quick leg into the city. At last she hit the gas and took a deep, cleansing breath at the same time.

Fixing her vision at the very top of her glasses so the fogged part would not be in her way, she threaded her way over the bridge and then through the one-way streets of Charleston until she turned right off Calhoun onto Meeting Street. Then she took another deep breath and relaxed. She had made it with time to kill. *Cool.*

An hour after she had left the island, she was parked at the top of the garage for the Omni Hotel, makeup retouched and a whole hour left before she got to meet the woman he had chosen. Would she be fat? Skinny? Probably, and beautiful, too, and rich. Rosie, knowing herself very well after all these years, was prepared for being early. She kept a book under the car seat for such times. It was better than letting her mind wander its twisted path, coming to its own depressing conclusions.

So she read a couple of chapters of some novel, and by the time it was 6:50 p.m., she had no idea what she had read, but she still felt good. Part of her mind pondered the exhilaration she was feeling when she usually would be a shaking mass of fat at the prospect of seeing an old boyfriend after driving into the city at night. Whatever the source of tonight's cheer, she was ready to go with it. As she stood waiting for the elevator down, she noticed a white Jaguar whisk up the ramp to the next parking deck. But James Brown was thumping in her head, and she gave the car no thought.

There he is! There he is! Rosie shouted to herself.

He stood with two rather tall, slim, dark-haired young men who each bore a strong resemblance to him. The trio stood in the lobby of the Omni at the bottom of the curving double stairway under the very flattering soft light of a huge chandelier. How did he get those tall boys? The wife must be a knockout, because Rob was of medium height and not the best-looking man in the world.

"Rob." She held out both arms to him. God, what if this wasn't him?

"Rosie!" He hugged her close with his head tilted back, just as she remembered. "Rosie, meet my sons. This is Matthew, and this is John. Peter is at home."

He must have gotten religion and reproduced the whole New Testament, Rosie thought.

There followed several minutes of small talk until Rob suggested that they repair to the sitting area in front of the huge fireplace and have a drink. More small talk. Rosie looked around the lobby and noticed the very subtle Valentine theme. A little red here and there. An ice Cupid on the buffet. Lots of chocolates set out in delicate dishes. She had forgotten all about Valentine's Day. She heard herself giving a quick rundown of her life and asking the right questions. The sons were very pleasant, taking after their father, Rosie thought. Where was *she*?

The hotel lobby was busy with people meeting people or passing through on their way to other parts of the complex. There were couples holding hands and a few children running about, giving off squeals of delight. The women Rosie saw were sleek and nattily dressed. Was the wife that one or the one walking in this direction? The men did not respond to the passing strangers, but Rob did order another round of drinks.

"Here comes Mom." One of the sons nodded in the direction of several people walking across the lobby. Rosie spotted her—silver hair, high heels, a well-tailored skirt and jacket, and of course, a slim figure. But that woman kept walking right on past their group.

"Sam, this is Rosie." Rob had his arm lightly around a dumpy, short person with chopped-off hair and beady eyes. Her floral dress rose and fell over waves of excess flesh around her waist. God, this was a shot of adrenaline to Rosie.

She jumped to her feet, her mouth open. "Hello, Sam, it's good to meet you. Welcome to Charleston."

"Yes, I'm sure." Sam's voice was dominated by nasal Yankee curtness. "It is time for our reservations in the Garden Room." As she spoke, she set off a ripple of motion all the way down her many chins.

The men instantly rose, and the group followed the ample figure as it stomped through the lobby to the dining room. He had married Petunia Pig! She looked just like Petunia Pig. Rosie had to cough so a giggle would not bubble up. Even the Hag got a little laugh. So he had not married a beautiful, slender woman but someone more like Rosie herself.

The maître d' settled them at a lovely table close to the rock garden. Crisp white linen fell into their laps.

"Did you have a good trip down?" Rosie asked.

All eyes went to Sam. "Too much traffic." Sam leaned on her elbows, causing the material across her upper arms to stretch across the bulges of flesh. Conversation ended. But Rosie, feeling that James Brown adrenaline, kept going.

"Sam, do you work—outside the home, I mean?"

"Of course," came the quick reply. "I am a doctor." She proceeded to give great detail about her work with diseases of the foot. Again Rosie gave a cough so she would not laugh out loud with delight. A foot doctor. A fat foot doctor! This was wonderful!

It was clear to Rosie who ran this family. The tension was tight, and so was Rosie, just a little. So she slipped her hand from her lap to Rob's knee and received a welcoming squeeze from Rob's hand. She remembered the time, so long ago, when she and Rob had driven down a two-lane country road with old oak trees stretching their arms over the drive. Rob had stopped his little car, and they had "necked" for a good long time. Oh, how wonderful was that memory. The more detail Sam gave about revolting feet, the higher up Rob's thigh Rosie's hand ventured. Rosie could almost smell the country air and hear the rustle of leaves on the long oak branches.

Rosie came up short when suddenly Sam asked, "What do you do, Rosie?" Rosie jerked her hand back so quickly that Rob gave a little start and grabbed his glass of water.

Dinner had been set before them, so Rosie took a bite of chicken and said, "I taught school. High school history, but I am retired now except for a little teacher-observation work now and then. That doesn't compare to feet." She couldn't help it—the laughter just poured out. She pushed her napkin up to her mouth, but the laughter kept flooding out. Tears ran down her face. Even the stiff sons began to giggle. Sam's expression did not change. She just continued to eat and eat.

"I'm sorry," Rosie managed. "I guess I'm a little nervous." She composed herself and gave a short history of her years in public education.

None of the Halseys spoke but Sam, so Rosie began to direct comments and questions to Matthew and John, who gave stilted replies. Rob said very little. It made her remember the meals she had shared with her daughters and Roy when he was sober. They had all talked at once, and they all had a say on each topic. If one of the Gatches had had a victory that day, that person got the praise earned. But the Halsey family was tense, and only one person had a right to speak. *Sad*, thought Rosie, *but not my business. Got my own sad businesses to mind.*

The dining room hummed with customers enjoying fine food. A string quartet played softly in the far corner. It was a beautiful evening. Rosie's hand was back under the folds of the tablecloth, stroking Rob's kneecap.

"Rosie," Sam asked in her fast northern twang, "what do you think has caused the schools in the South to do so poorly?"

Well now, Rosie could go on and on talking about the failure of schools. She loved to get on her soapbox and expound for hours. She had good ideas, one of which was the proliferation of children having children they could not take care of and expecting the schools and government to provide heaven on earth for their lazy butts. Rosie had perfected her argument to a refined, researched discourse, but tonight, with James Brown knocking around in her head and Petunia Pig sitting at the table, she gave a one-word response.

"Sex."

"*Sex?*" Sam's eyes opened wide. Her face began to flush. "Why does everything come back to sex? What in the world has sex to do with education?" She slammed her hand down on the table.

"Mom, Dad, may we be excused? We want to go to that little club we saw down the street." John and Matthew quickly stood up. They had heard this conversation many painful times before. "Nice to meet you, Rosie." And they fled.

The departure of the boys, timed with the arrival of dessert and coffee, enabled the conversation at the table to be diverted to more mundane things. Rob commented on the many changes in the old city. He liked the upbeat air that buzzed around the hotel. Sam nodded in agreement as she shoveled in cheesecake and fruit. For once Rosie found herself picking at her dessert and determined not to eat any more, just out of spite, so she leaned back in her chair and ran her hand back up Rob's thigh. Oh, this was fun! She could feel his response to her handiwork.

Sam suddenly leaned across the table to make a point, and Rosie froze. Did Sam see where her hand was?

No, thank God. Rosie had not heard what Sam had said, but she looked interested in every word. Her hand resumed its stroking. Rob was beginning to moan quietly, and his eyes glazed over.

"Rob! What is the matter with you?" Sam demanded. "You look sick."

Rob gave Rosie's hand a squeeze and then gently pushed it away. "I'm fine. Fine." His voice sounded a little short of breath. "Just fine."

"I have to go to the ladies'. I'll be right back." Sam rose and left the table, but Rob did not move.

They were silent until she was out of earshot, and then they began to laugh. Neither one could get a word out. Finally catching his breath, Rob gasped, "For a minute there I thought I would have to knock a glass of wine onto my lap." And he doubled over again.

Rosie was full of questions but could only giggle. "Tell me her daddy is very rich and you love her."

"Her daddy *is* very rich, and I once loved her." This set them off again. "I have so much to ask you and to tell you, but all I can do is sit here and laugh! Oh, I miss this."

"What? The thigh rub or the laughing?" Rosie blurted out.

"Both!" he almost shouted.

They saw that Sam was threading her way through the other tables back to them, so they forced themselves to quiet down and look serious. As Sam waddled past each table, the people at the tables made friendly sounds and then laughed. A mother quickly clamped her hand over her son's mouth to hush him. Heads turned to follow the path of Petunia plodding to her seat.

"Southerners are so friendly. All those people spoke to me." She flopped heavily into her chair. "Has the check come yet? Make sure you use the Gold Card to pay it." She stressed the word "Gold" for Rosie's benefit.

After the bill was paid, Rosie led the way back into the lobby.

"That was a beautiful meal. Thank you so much for calling me."

"Sam, I'll walk Rosie to her car. Why don't you go on up to the room? I know you're tired."

With a kiss in the direction of Rosie's cheek, Sam said, "Thank you for joining us. And Happy Valentine's. Be careful on that drive back alone." She held onto the word "alone" just a little longer than necessary. Then she turned to ascend the beautiful, graceful stairway with her ungainly gait causing her unflattering floral-print dress to swish from side to side. Her sturdy heels made loud clacking noises on the marble steps, causing heads to turn in her direction.

Noticing something dragging behind Sam, Rosie called out, "Oh, my God, Rob."

"Hush," Rob whispered as he grabbed her arm hard and waved up to Sam. "Good night, dear. I'll be right there. Don't say another word, Rosie. Just walk!" He almost ran them through the revolving doors to the courtyard. When they were hidden in the shadows, they looked back into the lobby to see Sam standing at the top of the curved stairs, lit by the soft, crystal chandelier, smiling down at the faces lifted up to her.

When the high voice of a child shouted out, "Mama, look at that lady's fanny! She has a tail!" Sam looked around and became horribly aware of the trail of toilet paper leading from the middle of the steps up to the top of her panty hose over her round rump. She flapped at the back of her dress and began to back up and out of Rosie's and Rob's sight—but not before Rosie could see Petunia's face turn a wonderful shade of blood red.

"Oh Rob, I have read about this happening, but I never thought it could be so wonderful!" Rosie had to lean against Rob to stay on her feet. She did feel a little sorry for Sam, but not *that* much.

They had to sit down on the edge of the fountain to catch their breath. People emerging from the lobby were all grinning and shaking their heads with glee. Rob splashed some water onto his face and flicked a few drops onto Rosie's.

"Oh Rosie, Rosie, this was a beautiful night. I love this city, and I miss the fun we had."

"I know," she replied. "Will I see you again? Within twenty years?"

"I don't know. I'm torn. We both have families." He kissed her lightly.

"Too late, too complicated," she said after the kiss. "I was worried about seeing you again. Scared, really. But it's like we just saw each other this morning, isn't it?" She could not quit smiling. "Rob, I want to walk to my car alone. I don't want to be alone with you in the dark. I want this evening to end on a high note."

He hugged her close. "I agree. I don't like it, but I do agree. Good night, valentine. It'll be less than ten years," he added softly. They both understood that more talk and a prolonged goodbye would accomplish nothing. They were friends from the heart.

She stood up, and they kissed again, and then slowly he walked back to the revolving door. The formally dressed doorman gave a slight bow as Rob turned to wave to Rosie, who, in a very loud voice, called, "I bet you don't get any!" James Brown was still in her head.

Rosie floated back to the island on clouds. Not even the opened bridge over the Ashley bothered her. The construction mess was a snap, and the strobe lights of oncoming cars did not faze her. Even the misty drizzle that kept the windshield streaky didn't bother her.

She wondered what went on in the hotel room after Rob returned. *I bet it was hell on wheels*, she thought. She felt a little sorry that Rob would receive the brunt of Petunia's wrath but knew that he was not without experience. His children were handsome and very well mannered. Rob had done well, whatever the price he had had to pay. After all, he was married to a doctor—a foot doctor! And the laughter started all over again. She and the Hag could both get a hoot out of the night.

"He called me *valentine*," Rosie whispered to Hades later as they went to sleep. "Valentine. He has the softest lips I have ever kissed.

Easter

2015

*S*pring turned the Low Country into a fairyland. The air was soft. Every tree, bush, and flower showed off its best dresses. Purples hung from the old oaks, pinks and reds lounged around all the yards, and yellows and light blues winked up from the bright green grasses. It all created a dreamland of color and perfumes. Birds sang all day. Bunnies hopped from under lacy ferns.

Rosie was on her deck finishing some school paperwork when her cell rang. It was the cute older couple, the Antonios, who lived next door. They had become good friends even though the Antonios were Yankees who had fled the mess of the big northern cities.

Maria's nasal voice barked over the phone: "We thought we would go to town for dinner and then maybe stop by John's for a beer. Want to join us?"

How did these Yankees know about John's, Rosie wondered? She had long gotten over the phase of feeling her stomach tighten every time John's bar was mentioned. But it still rattled her a little.

"Sure," Rosie replied. "Sounds good."

Two hours later all three friends pushed back from the table at Henry's Grill and declared it had been a delightful meal, a stupendous steak, no dessert, please. They walked the short distance to Big John's, where John slid three draft beers down the smooth bar top to their waiting hands. When John had seen Rosie, he had winked at her and gotten a small smile in return. He seemed to wonder whether he should say something, but the flood of customers coming into the place distracted him. Rosie was struck with the smell of the bar, the smoke that created a blue haze, and the mingling odors of mold and urine—John had never updated his restrooms because the men loved to challenge each other as to who could break the ice. A block of ice stood over the drain in the men's room, as in olden days. And of course there were beer and sweat to mix in their familiar odors.

Soon the trio moved to a booth with cracked green plastic seats. They had to shout to hear each other. A very tall man with black hair and big-rimmed glasses plopped down by Maria, who gave a look of surprise and gave him a huge hug. Just as Maria was shouting out introductions, a group of happy, half-drunk sailors rolled in the door, and the noise level rose to where no one could hear any names and Maria shrugged her shoulders and giggled.

After three beers and a lot of talk that none of the four really understood, Tony rose and announced it was time to get back over the river and into bed. While no one really heard that, they understood, and the women joined him for the walk back to the car. They waved goodbye and left the tall man chatting with a group of drinkers.

Back in the car, Maria said, "I am glad we ran into George. He works in the office next to me. Just divorced, lonely, sexy. Huh, Rosie? Huh, Rosie?" She gave Rosie a knowing grin and wagged her eyebrows up and down. Rosie did not answer, as she had barely noticed George anyway.

* * *

Did you have fun? Have fun? Hades asked as she danced around Rosie's feet in her welcome-home display.

"Kinda," was the reply.

She met a man who gave her big dreams of a wild night in the sack, but, you know, that is a stupid dream. What man would want to put his thing in that thing? Just the thought makes me laugh. The Hag had floated into the bedroom and hung upside down from the light with a beer in her hand. Somehow the beer flowed up into her red, evil mouth.

Hades jumped as high as a little Chihuahua could, trying to snag that piece of dung. Her barks got sharper and sharper until Rosie picked her up. Still she shook with anger. Rosie kissed the little head and said, "Don't, little one. You can't stop her attacks, you know that. She wants to kill me someday. To break me into little pieces of pain. She is doing pretty good."

Too tired from all the beer to even try to make a box to shove the Hag into, Rosie just lay on her back in her bed and stared up at the vision on the ceiling. The Hag made a circle with the index finger and the thumb of one hand and ran the index finger of the other hand in and out of the circle, all the while laughing and laughing.

Easter was on its way. Hop, hop, hopping along. Rosie had loved Easter since she was a child. Her mother had made baskets for them until they were way past grown. Dyeing eggs, making a bunny cake, and eating jelly beans were just wonderful. Most of all Rosie had loved watching her children reach under their beds for the baskets the rabbit had left. Then they all went out to find colored eggs in the grass, on a car wheel, on a tree limb, in a shrub. Just plain joy. It had been almost as much fun when Polly had children and she watched them glow with Easter delight.

This year no one was coming. The Antonios were busy with their Catholic friends at church. Star was midwifing some million-dollar show dog; Polly's children were in a skit, so she could not leave; and Izzy was now in Haiti saving the world. Rosie knew they would all three dye eggs; that made her smile. So what to do, what to do?

Ahhh, she thought, *I know what I will do.* And she got busy.

"Be still." Rosie put the finishing touches on Hades and then lowered her into a big basket. Carefully she placed a pink towel over the basket before she placed her own headpiece on her frizzy hair. "And for God's sake, be quiet!"

Mistake. You are going to make a fool of yourself and scare the hell out of those old people. Stupid. The Hag was snorting so hard with pleasure she had to take a deep breath. *Remember the fat lady? Eh? You wrapped up in quilts at the art gala and those boys throwing things at you? I remember! Oh yes, a circus theme at the art gallery, and you let your sister talk you into being the fat lady. I could go on and on. You are so stupid. Fat lady!*

Rosie did not hesitate but strode into the lobby of the place-of-the-living-dead retirement home with the big basket on her arm. Sure enough, one old lady shrieked at the sight of her but then began to point and chuckle. "Look at the big bunny!" The old lady pointed to Rosie's head, which supported two huge pink ears that wiggled when she walked. "She even has a black nose and whiskers. Wake up, Ethel, and look." The old lady gave a strong nudge to Ethel, who was pretending to read the newspaper but was really snoring. "Have you ever? Ethel? Is it Easter, Ethel?"

Ethel jerked awake and produced a shrill scream. "Help me!" she screeched as she struggled to her swollen feet, newspapers scattering, and clomped down the hall. "It's the White Rabbit. Help!" Her shaking voice trailed off.

Rosie stopped in her rabbit tracks. She did not look that weird. She had on a nice pink warm-weather sweat suit and had long ears on her head. Maybe the nose was a bit much. The basket was beginning to move and make strange noises as it hung on her arm. A group of residents had gathered about the very large, long-eared creature.

"Don't let Ethel upset you, dear. You look great. I love it," someone said.

They all murmured appreciation of her efforts. "What's in the basket? Easter eggs?"

"Yes." Rosie got over the shock. "Yes, that's right, Easter eggs. Eggs." She gave the basket a shake, and it growled. "Oh my, I'm late, I'm late," she added with a twinkle in her eyes and hurried off toward the clinic.

"Look, Ethel!" shouted the old lady. "She has a fluffy tail. Ethel, Ethel, where are you, Ethel?"

Rosie carried the basket into the clinic and quickly walked past the nurses' desk and the blank faces attached to dried-up bodies that sat in the chairs in the little community area. She stopped at Ada's door, drew herself up to full rabbit height, and then hopped into her mother's room with her arms pulled up rabbit style, holding the basket in front of her.

"Here comes Peter Cottontail," she sang as she hopped, "hopping down the bunny trail." When she reached Ada's narrow bed, she reached into the basket and produced a snarling, snapping Hades, whose little body began whipping back and forth in Rosie's raised hands. "Here comes Peter Cottontail," Rosie kept singing. She turned around so her mother could see the huge cotton tail she had glued to her pants. Then she held Hades so her little cotton tail showed. Hades still snarled and struggled.

Ada was struck dumb. Her hand stopped in midair on its mission of carrying an M&M to her mouth. "Who are you?"

"It's me, Rosie, and Hades, your very own Easter bunnies." Rosie, as the pink rabbit, sat on the foot of the bed. The old lady would have rolled onto the floor from her weight if it had not been for the side rails. Hades sat stiffly in Rosie's grasp. Rosie began to pull Easter grass and candy from the basket and made a little colorful mound on Ada's legs.

"Oh, you are Rosie. Here, darling, give me a hug." Ada held her skinny arms up, and Rosie leaned over and gave her mother a hug. Ada smelled good, as usual. "Let me see the tail again."

Rosie hopped around and wagged her rump back and forth. She and Ada sat talking softly and enjoying the Easter feeling of being together. Ada had made a big to-do over Easter every year. She had made baskets for her three children even after the children had become middle-aged, with homes of their own. When they had been young, they had hunted hidden eggs every Easter morning. Nothing had been better than tiptoeing through the damp morning grass, hunting for bright eggs hidden in lumps of flowers or trickily concealed up in a tree branch. Rosie had made her own children hunt for eggs.

In the past it had been a wonderful morning. Everyone had loved it. They had had a big breakfast and then hunted eggs. As a result, Easter was a big event, and it was Rosie's favorite holiday. It was so much easier than Christmas. Less tension and more fun.

Hades had been dozing by Ada's knees. Suddenly she lifted her head and began to growl. Rosie jumped up, grabbing the little dog to her chest. But she was not fast enough to keep the creature from being spotted by the nurse who had just entered the room. The nurse stopped where she was, hands on her ample hips.

"That is a dog," she hissed through tight lips. "Dogs are not allowed."

Hades began to bark with gusto. *How dare that woman question what I am.* Her little body flew out of Rosie's hands and bounced onto the bed, where Ada slapped at her with feeble hands.

"What is that?" Ada quaked, having totally forgotten the previous few minutes.

The nurse stepped closer to the bed. Hades lunged at her, mighty fangs bared and lips pulled back. The nurse swung at the little Chihuahua as Rosie jumped in to rescue her baby. Rosie and the nurse collided while Ada kept slapping at the "thing" rolling around on her bed.

"What is it?" Ada asked over and over, her voice becoming hysterical.

"It's a dog!" the nurse snarled as she straightened up and adjusted the lopsided weave on her head.

"It's my dog!" Rosie squeaked. Her long ears were hanging under her chins. She managed to push them back up into her hair. "It's my dog, Mama." Rosie quieted the monster that Hades had become and quickly placed her back into the basket with the towel, willing her to stay still.

In the few seconds of confusion, Ada had transformed from the almost-sweet old mother into the angry, mean person Rosie dreaded. Rosie knew that her mother had had a very hard, sad life and that she was scared here, at the mercy of strangers. Old age was hell, she knew. But the child in her could never accept this biting anger. She had seen her mother like this most of her life. In fact the sweet mother was rare. Rosie hated the cold, hard look on Ada's face. It was like a mad dog tied to a chain. It barked and wanted attention, but each time a hand reached out to touch it, the dog bit.

The dog's owner loved the dog. The dog loved and needed the person, but something in the dog made it hurt whoever was kind enough to come to it. It pulled at its chain, wanting freedom, but was jerked back by the connection to the long-gone past. The chain might weaken for short times, but it always reformed and hardened into cold steel.

The room was hushed. Hades had been shocked into silence by the rough treatment and loud voices. The nurse was indignant. Her breath came in jerky little snorts as she brushed at her uniform. The big pink rabbit stood there with tears in her eyes. Only Ada seemed coherent. She pulled the bedspread up to her chin and reached for the tiny M&M container on her bedside tray. As she put a piece of candy through her thin lips and over the yellow teeth, she coldly eyed the nurse.

"It is time for my bourbon," she announced with the haughtiness of a born Charleston lady.

The nurse, happy to have a reason to leave the scene, swung her hefty body around and stomped out of the room. The hair weave wobbled with each step. The stomps could be heard as she stormed up the hall to complain, once again, about that mean old white lady.

"I'll drink that damn bourbon for her," Rosie heard her mutter to the charge nurse.

Rosie petted the scared little dog in the basket and looked at her mother. *I have driven for two hours, I made this getup, and all I wanted was for you to say, "this is nice" or "thank you." I wanted a mama. I wanted—hell, I want to get out of here*! All of these words stayed locked in the rabbit's small brain. Rosie looked at her mother, who was completely enthralled with the M&Ms and the approaching bourbon.

"I have to go, Mama. I want to get home before dark, and I have things to do tomorrow. I hope you enjoy the eggs and candy." Rosie reached down and straightened up the little Easter nest she had made on her mother's legs. "Happy Easter."

Ada reached a skeletal hand down to the dyed eggs. "Yes," she replied coolly, "you best get home before dark. Would you please do something with this stuff before you leave?" Her voice was dismissive.

Rosie placed the basket on the floor, giving Hades a little pat, and gathered up the eggs and candy. "Where would you like them, Mother?" Her voice was strong.

"You know we have had trouble with ants. Maybe you better put them in the trash." Ada waved to the can by the dresser. "Where is that nurse? They know I need that drink to increase my appetite. They do that on purpose." The last words came out with a sneer that drew her mouth down in the corners. Rosie rammed the beautifully dyed eggs and Easter candy into the basket with the dog.

"And Rosie"—Ada had assumed the expression of someone who smelled something deadly but didn't want to let on—"go out the back door. You know it is Sunday, and you have those funny clothes. I don't know why you do this. People dress here. Give me a goodbye kiss."

Rosie kissed the spotted cheek and stepped to the mirror. She straightened her long ears and then reached around to check her tail, which she found was still in place. Looking at her image, she wiped the tears from her eyes. *Are you ready for this?* she asked her reflected self.

Yes, came the reply from the basket. *Let me out, let me out.*

"Goodbye, Mother." Rosie reached into the basket and picked up her dog. The little cotton tail was still in place. She quickly reaffixed the ears and placed the little black rabbit on the worn tile floor.

"To hell with it. Let's go, dog."

After giving Ada a bow, the big rabbit strode from the room with a little rabbit making sharp tapping sounds on the hall floor as it hurried to keep up with its leader. Once away from the door to Ada's room, Rosie stopped and stood with her back pressed to the white wall. Her eyes again filled with tears.

Gotcha good, didn't I? Told you, I told you. Stupid. How old do you think you are? Four? The Hag was back, now armed with sharpened arrows to slowly prod into Rosie's torn heart for weeks to come. Rosie rubbed at her blackened rabbit nose while she closed her eyes tightly. She concentrated on the noises in the hall. There were voices speaking normally about church, someone yelled for a nurse, a football game sounded from the room of the only old male on the hall, and a disembodied drone announced over the intercom, "Bingo at 6:00 p.m. in the dining room."

You never learn. You—The Hag's raspy, condemning voice was cut short by a soft tug on Rosie's arm.

"Your little bunny is scared."

Rosie opened her eyes to look down through fogged glasses into a sweet pink face full of wrinkles and surrounded by wisps of grayish-red hair. The elderly woman wore a floral-print dress that fluffed out over the huge wheelchair that supported her very big girth. "You better pick her up," the kind voice added. She had silk flowers pinned to her head and a very sweet smile showing a few gaps where teeth used to be. She looked just like a huge, beautiful flower to Rosie.

Pick me up, pick me up. I may get squashed. The nervous little body danced at her feet.

A snort of high, stressed laughter bubbled out of Rosie's mouth. She scooped up Hades and pressed the smooth little head to her hot cheek. "Thank you."

The flower rolled her chair back a few feet so she could look Rosie up and down very carefully.

"You make me happy. I love Easter. I used to dress up like that for the children in my first-grade classroom. They always laughed and hugged me. I taught first grade for fifty years at Memminger Elementary in the city. Never married. Have no family, just the sweet memories of those precious children. May I hug you?"

Rosie bent over the old rose and sobbed into her powdered neck. Hades put a quick stop to that by squirming around and demanding attention.

"I'm sorry," Rosie mumbled. "It's just...it's just..."

"It's just fucking hell. This place is fucking hell. Is that what you mean?"

This time the giggle was for real. Rosie straightened up herself and the basket full of Easter goodies and the Easter dog. "Yes, wow!" The words had shocked her back to reality. "Here, have some eggs and candy." She filled the big floral lap with a mound of stuff.

"You know," the rose said as she bit into a jelly bean, "life is full of shit. Not one of those precious children has ever come to see me. Not one. The shit gets deeper as you get older in some ways; not all, but some, especially the body. But then"—she popped another jelly bean—"damn, it's better than checking the fuck out. Don't you think?" Her faded blue eyes gave a wicked twinkle. Abruptly she jerked her chair around and almost cut a wheelie as she sped down the hall, her flabby arms pumping like mad. "I shoulda flunked them all!"

With a refreshed sense of herself, Rosie put Hades back on the well-polished floor. The Chihuahua-rabbit looked around to make sure there were no big feet or runaway wheelchairs close by, and then she pranced up the hall behind Rosie, who was once again singing, "Here comes Peter Cottontail..." When Rosie reached the nurses' station, she sang even louder. The nurses smiled because it was rare that they dealt with anything but dirty adult diapers and the approach of the grim reaper. They could handle an insane rabbit. Hair Weave walked stiffly from behind the desk with a tray of medications that included a plastic cup of 90-proof bourbon. Even she cracked a smile.

Rosie kept singing as she shot her hand out and grabbed the little white cup that contained Ada's beloved bourbon medication from the tray held by Hair Weave. She downed it in one gulp and then returned the empty cup. Before anyone could protest, she turned to the dregs of what had once been active, loved humans but were now inhabitants of the terrifying la-la land of old age, and she resumed singing. She hopped from person to person, placing an Easter treat in each shaking hand. A couple of the ruined faces smiled, but most just remained blank, scared of the object placed in their hands. One just let the brightly colored egg roll onto the floor.

"Happy Easter to all," Rosie pronounced, and she continued on down the hall that led back out to the lobby. She was not about to drag her tail out the back door. She loved her pink sweat suit. It had cost a lot of money, and by damn, it was going out the way it came in—the main front door. With Hades darting around her feet with determined little taps, Rosie managed to walk out of the home with her ears high and a smile pasted onto her rabbit face.

Once in the car, with her Easter ears and tail stripped off, 102.5 blaring sixties rock and roll, and Hades behind her neck, Rosie tore out of the home's long drive. The car knew where to go. The car knew that when it was empty, it wanted to binge on gas, and when Rosie's soul was empty, she wanted to binge on FOOD. It went straight to Burger King. The girl at the window handed the rabbit a bag containing a quarter pounder, fries, wings, and a real coke. The rabbit almost drooled, and the girl in the window stepped away quickly. As soon as she had a mouth full of fries, Rosie burst into tears. Racking sobs caused the dog to raise her head from her own plain hamburger.

Humans, the tiny brain thought to itself, and she went back to devouring her food.

What can I say? said the Hag. *Let's see...you are fifty-one, fat, dressed like a bunny, sitting alone in your car at Burger King, and stuffing your mouth. Need more? You have tried all your life to get something that is not there. It is not there. You will never get it. Grow up. Stupid.*

Shut up, shut up, I'll kill you, Hades growled over her burger.

Rosie placed her tear-stained glasses on the dash and struggled to get the Whopper in position to bite. Eating and crying. It sounded like a country song, but it was Rosie's life. Open her soul for love, get hurt, eat. Maybe she could just eat and eat and skip the hurting part. The sobs dried up as the taste of the food flooded her senses. For the next several minutes, the sounds of eating filled the car. Rosie licked the last of the special sauce off her fingers and stuffed the food wraps and the cups back into the meal sack, which she tossed onto the backseat floor.

"That's for you, my brother. Yes, I am an FFQ." Rosie felt she should explain to the Chihuahua what FFQ meant, even if the little dog was not very interested. "Every time your uncle nears my car, he begins to sniff. Then he checks the floorboards. 'Are you still an FFQ?' he'll ask. FFQ—get it, Hades? Fast food queen. Do I still enjoy the sinful pleasures of the drive-through window to clogged arteries and death? Yes, we do, little dog. Yes, we do."

I think I would tell him to just f-f-fuck off. Hades began to snore.

Rosie slammed the car into gear, pulled out of Burger King, and pointed in the direction of I-26W and home. Rosie noticed, as she looked into the rearview mirror to check before merging onto the interstate, that she was smiling. Where had this habit of finding something silly to occupy her mind when she was threatened by deadly serious events come from? Once she had laughed out loud when her drunk husband had forced her to her knees to beg forgiveness for weeding the garden without his permission. It was just so dumb. But wherever it came from, she liked it.

Rosie set the cruise control at eighty. If only she had remembered to stop by the library before leaving home and pick up a book on tape, her mind would have been occupied and not open for an hour of self-flagellation. The Hag wasn't necessary for this. The monotonous highway lay open before her car like an invitation to a long, boring pity party. She set the dial on the classical station.

She agreed with what the Hag had taunted her with in the hallway. She was looking for something that her brain knew was not there. But the child in her—or maybe it was just plain madness—drove her to constantly seek the Beaver Cleaver mother who lived only in the imaginations of screenwriters responsible for creating a fantasy world that caused millions of people to spend their whole lives in search of the perfect mother. Her brain knew that. She knew she wasn't a perfect mother to her three daughters. She expected her children to accept that. So why did she spend so much energy in search of the unattainable? So much pain. Did she like the pain? Was it a habit?

If she had worn a Chanel suit, pumps, and pearls and carried a pair of white gloves to the home, her mother would have glowed. Ada would have insisted on eating in the big dining room so she could have shown off the suit, not shown off Rosie. So why hadn't Rosie done that? Yeah, a Chanel in size eighteen—did they even make them that big? But she could have worn a simple dress and taken her mother a small, polite Easter basket. Kept her voice down. As many times as Rosie had sat on a shrink's couch or a priest's sofa and poured out her heart, she thought there should have been an answer. An answer to why she could not do anything in a simple way. It always had to be a little different, a little over the top, or not at all. Nine times out of ten, her actions brought her nothing but pain. The pain resulted in eating and drinking and getting fatter. Which brought more pain and more visits from the Hag. Although she never could find a reason for this destructive pattern, she was beginning to recognize it.

Rosie pondered for the last hour home. *If I can see it and describe it, why can't I stop it? Why am I doomed to repeat it like a character in some Greek tragedy? I'm like Prometheus and his ever-returning liver.*

She needs a rabbit shrink, Hades muttered to the car and resumed her nap.

July

2015

*I*t was hot as only the Low Country can be hot. Heavy, sweaty, sticky, buggy. Hazy and lazy. Rosie had gotten raw peanuts from the Pig on her way to the condo. Last night she had boiled them in a big pot with a lot of salt. When they were done, she let them cool in the salty water, drained them, and put them in the fridge for the next day. Now, sitting in the swing with the big bowl of peanuts between her knees and a cold beer balanced on the swing arm, Rosie gently pushed the swing using her bare feet. Hades dozed in the sun but kept an ear cocked for interesting noises.

The day was beautiful but hot; boats were bobbing at the docks, waiting for people who were coming for the weekend. Rosie let her eyes rove the marina for the little white-and-brown boat. *No*, she told herself. *So what if he's not here? Still a nice time, just for me. But a night in the V-berth might be fun.* She felt a quiver deep in her tummy. *Quit that*, she quickly scolded herself. *Just quit it.*

She stood up, placing the bowl in the swing, grabbed her beer, and walked to the edge of the grass, where it met the planks of the dock. No little white-and-brown boat. Rosie had turned to go back into the condo when Hades cut loose with a joyous bark and a lot of high-pitched squeaks. Just as Rosie saw that Jigger was the cause of such dog happiness, a pair of strong arms wrapped around her waist from behind and lifted her off her feet. She began to squeal, Steve laughed, and the dogs howled with glee as beer flew in every direction.

"Where did you come from?" a breathless Rosie gasped. "Where is your boat?"

For an answer, Steve swung her around and planted a big, penetrating kiss on her lips. She put her arms around his neck and felt his sandy beard dig into her face. His left hand pushed her lips into his eager mouth, and his right hand grabbed her left buttock. Slowly he moved his hips back and forth until she felt his desire become as hard as a brick. Her knees weakened; she staggered back a little, gasping for breath.

"Oh my God, oh my God." Her knees kept bending, and she felt for the swing. Finally her skin made contact, and she crashed down on the swaying seat. Her motion pulled Steve awkwardly on top of her as they were still joined at the mouth, their minds and bodies filled with animal urges of which we will not speak.

Their tangled bodies were too much for the innocent swing, and it tilted, causing the chains to let go from the ceiling so the whole load was thrown backward onto the cement patio. Arms and legs flailed about, heads cracked, peanuts flew up into the air, the porcelain bowl splintered into hundreds of shards, dogs barked, people hung over the upstairs balcony, and other people ran over from the dock. Having seen the flying peanuts, seagulls began to gather.

What fun, what fun, cackled the Hag. She laughed so hard she almost cried. *Told ya, told ya.*

Rosie had forgotten all about her this trip to the water. But there she was. Rosie laughed with the Hag, for once, because it really was a funny scene. That happy laughter made the Hag mad, and she withdrew in a huff of snorts and vague mutters of returning.

Rosie and Steve began to look around as people stepped in to help pull them to their feet. Hands brushed them off, and as soon as they discovered no blood or broken bones, people began to giggle and laugh. "Oh my Lord," Rosie said, and Steve countered with "Well, Gawd damn. Girl, you can pack a kiss, Gawd damn."

The crowd melted away. Steve pulled the broken swing up next to the condo while Rosie dealt with the shards of glass. Jigger and Hades took care of the peanuts, as did a few brave gulls.

"Have you got plans?" he asked.

"No."

"Good. Come down to the boat." He pointed way over behind the big deep-sea fishing boats. "I'm over there. Shower, but no makeup or underwear. And no dusting powder or jewelry." He turned, motioned for Jigger, and headed down the dock.

Rosie stood there staring after him. "No jewelry?" she whispered to herself.

"It gets caught in my teeth," he answered over his shoulder. Then he wagged his tongue.

She flew into the condo, slid the glass door shut, and quickly pulled the curtains closed. Then she flopped onto the sofa and was not sure if she was crying with humiliation or giggling with anticipation.

Rosie stripped, enjoyed a steaming hot shower where she scrubbed and washed places that had not seen daylight in years and then toweled dry. She dabbed iodine on a couple of spots where she had pulled out sharp shards of porcelain. Dressing was easy with the rules Steve had set. Every time the Hag tried to butt in, Hades growled, and Rosie hummed. She was determined to stay happy and not doubt herself.

At last Rosie and the tiny Chihuahua started down the dock to the little white-and-brown boat. It was dwarfed in a slip between two huge fishing boats filled with law-yer types sipping Scotch and cleaning their fishing gear. Rosie scooped up Hades, who had been looking up at two gorgeous golden Labs with their heads hanging over the edge of their human's boat. Their shining fur ruffled in the gentle breeze, their tails waving like flags and their long pink tongues flapping over big white teeth.

Oh, why can't I look like that? Just a little? sighed the tiny dog to herself. Were there little Hags for little dogs?

Steve popped his head up and, with a big grin, said, "Welcome aboard." He helped Rosie over the side of the boat, tossed her bag down into the cabin, and gave her a bear hug. Jigger and Hades sniffed hello. The men on the big fishing boats hooted and whistled. "Let us descend into my lush yacht." Steve loosened his hold on Rosie and bounced down into the cabin. Rosie, not being as agile, turned so she could back down the short ladder to below. Hades watched from above.

"Don't bite me," Rosie said, recalling her disastrous first boarding of the little boat.

"Oh, I won't," replied Steve as he ran his hand up her right leg to check for underwear. "Good girl," he announced. Rosie gave a little gasp as his fingers moved across her nude bottom.

After landing firmly on the floor, Rosie reached up and lifted Hades down into the cozy cabin. The two dogs took off to parts unknown, yipping and sniffing. Steve placed her bag on a bunk and then put his index finger to his lips and made a *shhhh* sound. Slowly soft music came up to fill the candlelit cabin with romantic sounds that matched the gentle rocking of the boat. The salt air with a touch of engine grease filled her with excitement. Steve still did not speak. He pulled her to a small table he had set with two silver goblets and two long-stemmed crystal wine glasses. There was a plate of little crackers and pieces of cheeses and meats. With great flair, Steve poured red wine into the crystal glasses.

Rosie took a long sip. Steve nodded toward the silver chalice by her right hand. She gave him a questioning look, as they were still not talking. He nodded again, and she moved forward to look into the chalice. She reached in and pulled out something red. Now using two hands, Rosie unfolded the red thing and held up a pair of vintage red panties with lace. Steve gave a bad-boy smile as she stepped into the panties and pulled them up under her short dress. They fit just right!

The Hag rarely showed herself; instead, she usually rattled in Rosie's brain. But tonight she could not resist this beautifully set scene to sow her poisoned seeds of self-serving sadness and despair. Her mean face, floating in a dark cloud right over Steve's head, resembled the face of the old woman in the house of the living dead. But the Hag was far more evil looking. Rosie froze as the red wine burned down her throat and then settled in her tight stomach.

Oh darling, snarled the face, *how much do you weigh? Is your girdle fastened? What happened to your fuzz—I mean hair?* She gave a long, dark giggle. The scurry of little feet brought both dogs into the cabin and under the table.

I will kill her. Kill her, the tiny black dog snarled, and she backed up to Rosie's feet to protect her. *Leave her alone, you witch. Let her live and enjoy. Go to hell.*

Rosie bent down and pulled the warrior dog to her chest and snuggled her face in next to the dog's face. "Thank you, little one, my friend, my strength. Here, have some meat." She fed Hades a few treats and threw a couple down for Jigger. Steve just stared, not knowing about the battle that had been fought and won. There was no sign of the Hag.

Rosie stood up and raised her chalice high. "Come on, lover boy." She grabbed his hand and jerked him to his feet.

He laughed deep in his chest and pulled her into his arms. "Come to Daddy." He led her to the wide V-berth and then began to remove her short T-shirt dress. As the smooth cloth slid over her tender breasts, her nipples hardened. Steve held her arms over her head, entangled in the shirt. With one hand, he encased her wrists, and with the other, he rubbed her aching breasts. Slowly he inched her backward into the V of the berth and pushed her down onto the rumpled sheets of the hard mattress. Her shaking legs were on each side of the V. Steve picked up her left leg, gently bent her knee, and lifted her foot up to the low ceiling. Here he hooked her toes over the narrow beam that served as a rib to the boat. He did the same with her right leg. The last thing Rosie remembered hearing was the unzipping of his shorts. Oh, she did hear someone singing, "Oh, sweet mystery of life, at last I found you."

The rising sun gave the marina a beautiful, soft glow. The marsh grass, tipped a pale pink with the sun's rays, danced in the gentle breezes. Water rippled around the boats tied at the floating docks. Dolphins rode the incoming tide. It was a beautiful Carolina morning.

Rosie sat in the cockpit, wrapped in a soft blanket. She watched Steve walking back to the little white-and-brown boat. He had walked the dogs and gotten take-out breakfast from the ship store. Both dogs liked to sniff around the big oak trees with moss waving in the soft air that hung over the dock. The big fishing boats had long left to cast their lines into the open sea, so the little boat was alone at the dock. The trio of man and dogs bounced a little on the floating ramp to the boat. He handed her the coffee and then lifted both dogs in his big hands and stepped aboard.

They did not speak, just sipped the hot coffee. The Chihuahuas, worn out from their adventure on land, found a spot of sun on the bow and fell asleep. The warm sun, salty air, gentle slapping of the stays against the mast, and cawing of seagulls all added to the unreal, romantic dream into which Rosie had allowed herself to slip. This would last forever and ever, amen.

Steve had sat down beside her, and his hand, still warm from the coffee cup he had handed her, nudged the blanket over her stomach a little. It found an opening and slowly crept down to the now achingly swollen spot between her determinedly clenched thighs. They both sipped lukewarm coffee. Her thighs, still sticky from last night, slowly parted. His eyes focused on the clouds in the sky, but his skilled fingers found their way to her awaiting volcano. Her eyes closed, and her head went back to rest on the deck rail. Rosie's body had begun to shake and quiver with quiet waves of pleasure when she felt something cold drip onto her face. No, she would not stop this pleasurable wave of—*drip, drip.* She opened one eye a bit and then screamed. The big furry face of a golden retriever was hanging over her; a long pink tongue almost touched her hair. Its bright eyes moved back and forth as the pink tongue swiped its wet nose.

Rosie's hands flew to her face as her head rolled from side to side only to find a big golden paw at each ear. In covering her face, she had let go of the blanket wrapped around her, so when she shot up off the bench in horror, she stood in all her splendor, clad in only a pair of red panties. Everyone froze.

"Beauregard! Beauregard! Come here now!" Beauregard stood with his hind feet on the floating dock and his front paws on the stern rail where Rosie had rested her head. "Jesus Christ, dog, come here." The shout came from up the dock, where a red-faced man stood waving his arms. From the sunny bow came the sharp barks of the little dogs who wanted in on what was happening. Beauregard thought it was wonderful fun, so he joined in the noise with his loud woofs. All the commotion drew a small crowd of people from other boats and from the ship store.

Rosie began to scream. Steve at last did something. He threw the blanket around Rosie and then doubled over with laughter. Rosie flew into the cabin and threw her dress on, covering her panties. She scrambled back onto the deck, grabbed her dog, gave Steve a hard kick in the rump, and stepped onto the dock, where Beauregard jumped up on her in delight. She began to run as best she could with a pack of dock dogs who had bounced over to investigate the noise swirling around her feet.

Rosie stopped short in the midst of the dogs and the laughter from everywhere. It was funny. She began to chuckle, completed the walk of shame, and asked for permission to board. Steve wiped his eyes and opened his arms to welcome her back. She stepped onboard and fell into his arms. The audience clapped with joy and wandered off to talk about the unbelievable scene they had seen. The little boat rocked with joy in the rising tide.

Halloween

The Low Country never dressed in bright autumn colors. Here and there stood a yellow or gold tree. The ginkgoes always showed off in their dresses of bright-orange fanlike leaves. Late October was usually crisp with bright sunlight. Sometimes it was downright hot, and the AC would need to run all day. This October day, Rosie loved this flat, marshy Low Country. The drive down from Mount Pleasant to Maybank Highway had been quick, and Main Road was moving well since the bridge had been completed.

With Hades tucked behind her neck, Rosie drove at a moderate speed so she could look through the trees to see what little change in color there was. The moon roof was open, and every now and then, Rosie stuck her arm up and waved a wiggly finger greeting to whoever happened to catch her eye. Make them wonder who that was who knew them but they hadn't recognized. As the little country churches and stores sped by, Rosie thought through her plans for the next few days. Her plans included...nothing. In a way that was scary, but then it was also a relief.

The past few weeks had been very tense. At work she was filling in for a teacher who was on pregnancy leave for this semester, which was stressful. God, she hated those smart-assed teenagers whose aim in life was to remain as dumb as dirt, as high as kites, and as horny as toads. It used to be that that type of student was the minority, but not anymore! The kids who actually wanted an education had long since fled to private schools or simply given up and joined the flow to a lifetime of cable TV and government-issued checks.

But the administration demanded high test scores from kids who came to school with minds as blank as clean sheets and left the same way. How in the hell could a teacher influence a child whose world thought the most important thing in life was to out-reproduce the farm animals while out fighting everyone from Granny to the pimp on the corner? Goddamn it, a faculty of middle-aged females could not take a student who could not read or write but had been promoted anyway and force that student to be successful on standardized tests. What were the teachers to do, hold guns to the empty heads? Hell, why not? That was the accepted behavior in most of the homes the little darlings came from. But if test scores were not improved, jobs were on the line.

Quit it. Quit it, the little black dog shouted. *Your neck is getting tense. The box, the box, put the school in the box. Remember? Dr. Boatwright and his box.*

"OK, you're right." Rosie took a deep, cleansing breath and forced her mind to picture a rather big box to force the whole school system into—yes, there, get in there, you idiots. *Don't forget you are driving!* she shouted to herself. Slam—the box closed, and Rosie was sure she would not think of that problem for a few days at least.

Would the white-and-brown boat be there with Steve waiting for her? She was ready. The few hours with him last July had been terrific, but she had not heard a peep from him since.

And you never will! The Hag had appeared, loaded for bear.

Shut up! Quit it!

You'll never see him again. If he is docked there, he will hide from you. He ain't stupid, fatty.

Leave her alone!

My God, I am alone in the car, Rosie thought, *and I can't follow the conversation.*

Alone? sniffed the dog, insulted.

You'll always be alone. And old.

Rosie slowed the big Taurus to turn into the Big Pig. *Both of you shut up.*

It took her only about twenty minutes to grab what she needed. Merlot, cheese and crackers, TP, OJ, and instant coffee would do for now. Standing in line to check out, she noticed the witches and bats hanging from the ceiling. Halloween. She had forgotten the holiday, but she snatched a bag of candy corn from the stand and threw it in with the other stuff. The activity cleared her head, so when she slid back behind the wheel, she felt much better.

By five o'clock Rosie was sitting in the swing on the brick patio of the condo, looking out at the expanse of dark water and into the clear, darkening sky. Wine in hand. Dog in lap. Cheese in mouth. Heaven. The air was cool and sharp. She could see lights twinkling in the homes way across the dark marsh and a few glowing portholes on the boats at the dock. The dark felt friendly. As usual she did not mind being alone. No one was home in the condo to the left or upstairs. The condo across the little patch of grass to the right was also dark. This was a vacation spot; this was not a place to be afraid. At least Rosie had never been afraid there. Not yet.

Rosie let Hades gently down from her lap so she could patter around in the grass for just the right spot. There, she found it and was quickly ready to call it a night. Rosie heaved her bulk out of the swing, gathered the leftover food (there was very little of that!), and ushered the dog inside.

"We won't do much tomorrow, old girl," Rosie told the sleepy dog. "Maybe walk on the beach and then go out for lunch. Maybe get a pumpkin from the Pig and carve an ugly face."

Fine. Fine. Good night. Hades circled twice, settled down, and immediately began snoring.

Rosie read until six o'clock and then put down the story about the Victorian Egyptologist and turned back the covers on the twin bed. It was good to be here at Seabrook. She had needed a change. She had even managed a quick visit to the house of the living dead to spend a little time with her mom. It had been a sweet visit, no complaints or fussing.

Now it was just the dog and her. She could hear footsteps on the wooden planks of the dock as people returned to their boats for the night. Other tourists meandered up and down the dock after they had dined at the little upscale café at the main dock. She liked the noise of feet and soft voices mixed with the clang of masts and rigging moving in the wind as the boats shifted with the tide.

No little boat. I told you so, sneered the Hag with a cruel laugh.

Shut up. Rosie was determined to force the Hag out of her soul and into the locked box in the back of her mind. Move over, schools. Rosie had worked hard over the years to rid herself of depressing thoughts and flashbacks to her sad childhood and her terrible marriage. Each month was better and better, but still there were a lot of setbacks. Just then her cell rang.

"Hello?" Rosie was happy for the distraction of her brother's voice. "Bro, I am so glad you called."

"Have you eaten yet?" Rosie could hear traffic behind his voice. She really had not thought about a real meal all day. "Jimmy wants to go fishing, and he needs me to help with the boat. I'll be at the condo in about twenty minutes."

Rosie jumped up, forgetting about the Hag. She showered and quickly pulled on a decent pair of jeans and a soft green sweater. Her hair curled and frizzed in the still-humid air, but a little makeup helped some. By the time William arrived, she looked decent and was mentally fortified for the weight remarks she was sure to endure.

They walked up the dock, dodging children dashing about in all sorts of Halloween costumes. There were even a few strippers and gangstas making a show tonight. Brother and sister were quietly chatting about the various boats rocking at the piers, and they had a good laugh, as always, at the huge boat that Jimmy could not handle and that cost about $50,000 a year just to keep in its rental slip. William and Jimmy had been roommates in college centuries ago and had been bosom buddies over the years. Rosie pictured them running over smaller boats that they never saw and then spending the night way up the Edisto, stuck on some oyster bank with alligators giving them the hungry eye. She knew they would return full of beer, red from the sun, and talking about the whale that got away. But right now William held the door to the bar open for Rosie to enter.

They were seated by the big window that overlooked the parking lot, ordered their meals, and continued chatting. Rosie noticed William staring out the window and watching a big white car pull up. The Jaguar slid into a parking space like a prowling cat, and a very tall man oozed out from behind the steering wheel.

"I know him," said Rosie as the man stepped through the doorway and passed their table.

William, who had never met a stranger, spoke as the man got even with his chair. "That is a beautiful steed you have there." He pointed to the white car. Rosie, still oblivious to who exactly he was, said, "My brother is a car worshipper...I think I have met you before."

The tall man stopped midstride and said, "Thank you." He proceeded to tell William all about how he got the car, how he tuned it, how he waxed it, and on and on. William indicated for the man to sit down, and as the man folded his long legs, he turned to Rosie and said, "I think we met at Big John's, but it was so noisy I did not catch your name. I am George T. Beck."

Rosie froze. The Hag laughed in her head. Good southern manners won out, and Rosie put her hand out and murmured, "I am Rosie Gatch." *The car,* she thought, *I should have picked up on the car. What a dunce.* A tense silence descended over the table. *Should I walk out? Should I thank him?* Rosie's mind whirled. Thank God for brothers.

"May I buy you a beer?" Always the good host, William took over. Maybe it was the Hag or just nerves, but Rosie began to sputter into a laugh that bubbled out of her like a roar. George, who looked like he rarely laughed out loud, found himself chuckling, William, trying to remain a gentleman, had tears running down his cheeks. What a horrible situation. There was nothing to do but scream, fight, or laugh. They all chose laughter.

The waitress, setting down the mugs of beer, asked, "What's so funny?" That set them off again, and so she left, and the trio at the little table gulped down their drinks, trying not to choke. None of the three had ever been in such an awkward position. They stared into their beer mugs for a few seconds, each hoping the others would say something. George began to push away from the table and rise to his feet.

"Don't. Don't go," Rosie muttered. He stayed. Rosie had done all she could not to see him or meet him during all the mess with Roy's death, but now she really wanted to talk to him. She surprised herself.

"Oh look, there are Jimmy and his wife, just walked in." William spoke a little too loudly but with great relief. "Let me go speak to them about tomorrow. Going fishing. Good to meet you, George, kind of strange. I must go for a second." With a scrape of his chair, he was gone, leaving the two people left at the table in a conundrum about what to do.

After a few minutes in which they both drank from their mugs, George asked, "Why do you want me to stay?"

"I'm not sure." The Hag rattled in her head, but Rosie refused to let her speak. "I think I am just curious. I never knew whether to curse you or write you a thank-you note. I even bought a box of thank-you notes, but none were right."

"Thank me?" His thick black eyebrows rose.

"Yes. Roy was a mean drunk, and I had dithered for years about leaving or murdering him. He passed out once at supper, and I gave it a long thought, the idea of holding his head in his soup till he drowned. You know, death by split pea."

When the waitress plopped down two hamburger baskets, they both had forgotten they had ordered. Rosie found she was very hungry and tucked right in. George watched her for a couple of seconds and then picked up the little cup of ketchup by his fries. With a loud slurp, he sucked down all the ketchup and gave Rosie a long look as he wiped his mouth with the back of his huge hand. "I love ketchup." That broke the tension. Then he picked up his hamburger and demolished it in four bites.

William was long gone back to the condo while George and Rosie talked and talked. He was at Bohicket just to ride around in his Jag and was headed back to town. Soon the blinking bar lights told them it was time to leave. Rosie forgot to worry about her ample tummy as she left the table—that dawned on her later. George held the door open for her and ushered her out with his warm hand on her waist. Her knees went weak.

"I'll walk you back." He led her around the bar and away from the white Jaguar to the wooden walkway that ran in front of the condos.

"It's not far," she said. "What do you do?" Rosie then asked the tall man. She came up to his armpit, and she liked that.

"I am a freelance reporter for a newspaper chain. I look for interesting events and people and do a story and take a few pictures and send it in. Luckily I don't have to go into my office often. The editors may like my article or not. I do OK."

The tide was high and reflected stars and moonlight. A soft breeze caused a gentle slapping of the tall sailboat masts. They walked more and more slowly. "Well, here I am. That is William's condo right there." And she pointed to the sliding glass doors with the tan curtains. A tiny black head poked out from under the curtains.

George took both her hands in his. "I know this is strange, but I want to see you again. Will you meet me at the bar for a drink tomorrow night?"

Rosie looked down at his hands. They were big, his fingers long and thick. Her hands were engulfed. She gazed at his thumbs and wondered whether the old wives' tale was true. A delicious chill ran up her legs. "Yes," she almost shouted.

Hades ran around and around Rosie's feet when she walked into the condo. She picked up the dog and kissed her head. *Don't do that. Don't do that. You are late and you are up to something. I can tell. I can tell.*

And another one bites the dust, the Hag said. *You have the hots for your husband's killer? How nuts can you be? Oh God, this is just wonderful. Fun. Fun.*

"Shhh, you will wake William," Rosie whispered as she tiptoed past the snoring and snorting form on the sofa and went into the bedroom. Once in bed Rosie went right to sleep and dreamed of little white-and-brown boats and white Jaguars.

The next morning, after straightening up the blankets on the sofa and other odds and ends, Rosie wrapped a throw around herself and settled in the swing with a hot cup of coffee and Hades sniffing around. She pondered the past few months. Roy dead. Moving. Steve. Working. Was there a God? Who was this George? Where did the Easter Bunny live? How old was Gee? She got more coffee and continued to think about how much had happened to her in the past year. Her children had had no crisis lately, but she had not heard from Izzy in a few weeks. And she had gotten laid in a glorious manner not too long ago.

About five o'clock, as the tide was coming in, she saw Jimmy's massive boat coming up the creek. *They will smash it into that other boat and sink. They can't dock that thing.* The Hag was smug. For once Rosie agreed with her. As the boat got closer, a small speedboat flew out into the creek and up to Jimmy's ship. Within a couple of minutes, the two men on the big boat got into the speedboat, and the two younger men from the little boat took charge of the big boat. Soon the little boat docked right in front of the condo, and William and Jimmy crawled out. Jimmy headed home on unsteady feet, and William tottered into his condo and fell on the sofa. The big boat found its slip and slipped in as smooth as silk.

"Did you see us dock? Man, we are good for two old fogies," William bragged.

"Oh, I saw that tradeoff. How much did that cost?" They had a good laugh.

"I am going to shower and sleep till sunup and then head back to Virginia," William said, heading for the bathroom.

"I have a date," Rosie said with a bit of pride, "with George. I have to meet him in a little while, so I might not see you before you leave. Give me a hug."

William put his arms around his sister, who immediately complained that he smelled of old-man sweat and fish. He returned, "Are you still an FFQ?" They parted with smiles and love.

Rosie went to dress with the help of Hades. *Don't overdo it. Just jeans and a sweater. Sweater.*

No sweater. It will just add to your bulging tummy, the Hag countered. *Wear something else.*

Sweater.

No sweater.

"Oh God, will you shut up?" Rosie screamed in her head. She pulled on jeans and a light blue sweatshirt and pushed the sleeves up. She added a dangly necklace and a little blush and lipstick. "Hades, wanna go with me?"

The little dog danced with excitement and stuck her tongue out at the Hag, who turned her back. Rosie put the leash on, and as she passed the sofa, she gave her clean, snoring brother a pat on the head. He grunted.

Rosie and Hades took their time walking up the dock to the bar. Hades found a lot to sniff, and Rosie did not want to be early. Both of them glanced around for the little white-and-brown boat, but they didn't tell each other that they did. There were still a few children running around in their Halloween costumes, mothers not far behind. Rosie stood at the fence that kept people, drunks, and dogs from rolling off the walkway and into the muddy water below. She put her elbows on a fence post and her head in her heads and took in the ever-amazing sunset, just like an old Selznick movie. It was more beautiful than a movie. Purples, golds, and yellows washed the marshes and the creek. Condo and boat windows reflected the sparkle. Hades was not impressed and pulled on her leash. *Let's go, let's go.*

She picked up Hades as they walked into the crowded, loud bar. She made her way to a small table by the big window, passing a table full of men with two big goldens sitting at their feet. *Oh God, please don't let them be the people from that big boat*, Rosie thought. *Don't let them say anything about my red panties.* The men did not look up, but the goldens looked her up and down, and she could have sworn they smirked knowingly. Hades felt it too and gave a soft growl.

He is not coming. Told you so, didn't I? You idiot.

Rosie ordered a beer and some chips. Hades sniffed around under the table, keeping an eye on the know-it-all goldens who wished they could talk and tell their story about the chubby woman and her little shrimp of a dog. Finding nothing of interest under the table, Hades got back into Rosie's lap and wondered where the mystery man was. Rosie was wondering the same thing. She ordered another beer and more chips.

Just as her second beer was set in front of her, the big sleek white Jag pulled up, and George unfolded from the front seat and walked into the bar. She waved to him, and he came right over.

"Sorry I'm late. I had a busy day and started out late." He signaled for the waitress, who came right over and took his order for a hamburger, fries, and a beer. Rosie indicated she wanted the same. "Have you been here long?"

Rosie totally forgot she had been waiting for half an hour. "No."

Hades sat up, gave George the once-over, and growled softly. *Not sure. Not sure.*

"Hush," Rosie whispered.

"What was that?"

"My little love, Hades. Hades, meet George." With introductions over, Hades settled back into Rosie's lap and dozed off.

The couple ate and drank and made small talk about their days. They slowly got into more personal talk. Talk about Roy and the accident could not be avoided. George said he would always feel guilty, and Rosie said she would always feel free. The event had affected both their lives in very different ways, but it connected them deeply. It was the first time George had seen someone die. He would always have that picture of Roy under the car wheel in his mind. Driving, for George, had always been an exercise in fun and freedom, but now there was a tinge of darkness over getting in his car for a spin.

"I better be going," Rosie said. "I'm leaving tomorrow. I have work Tuesday." She stood up and put Hades on the floor. The two goldens lifted their big, beautiful heads together and licked their black lips lasciviously. Hades lunged at the pair, who just ignored her and looked Rosie up and down. Hades's eyes bulged, and her terrible barking lifted her off her feet. Rosie had to pick her up.

"What was that with the dogs? I'll walk you." George joined her and guided her through the crowded room to the door, where he took her hand and did not let it go. Hades pulled at her leash and sniffed through the grass by the walk. The goldens were forgotten.

Rosie floated back to the condo with that huge hand around hers. When they reached her door, George pulled her close and wrapped his arms around her. Her face was pressed against his chest. He smelled so good! "Don't go in yet," he whispered. He led her to the swing, which William had repaired after a lot of questions and dirty insinuations.

They cuddled as the swing moved gently. A few boats moved down the creek with their lights twinkling like stars. Something scuttled in the bushes behind them, and they laughed and hoped it was not an alligator. Hades slept in Rosie's lap. It was a cool, clear, early-November night, a good night to talk in low voices and snuggle up close.

Thanksgiving

2015

Over the next couple of weeks, Rosie was very busy with the school. She told her neighbors about meeting George again, and this time she had learned his name! The neighbors were thrilled and asked her to bring him to church. Rosie told her sister about the lanky, sexy man and how they had worked out the strange connection between them. Karma, said Chick, karma. Star, Polly, and Izzy were more dubious but wanted their mother to be happy.

One morning as she was driving to work over that damned long bridge, a thought hit her. The Hag had been very quiet. In fact, she had been absent for a time. What was she planning? Rosie decided to let sleeping dogs lie and proceeded on to school. On the way home, she again thought about the Hag. *I will talk to Hades about it*, she thought, and she did.

Once home Rosie poured a glass of wine and sat on her sofa, with Hades at attention. Rosie explained to the little Chihuahua that the Hag had been absent for a while. Hades agreed. "What do you think about that?" Rosie asked. Hades scratched her right ear and licked both front paws while she pondered the question.

You. You. You are stronger. You are happier. You have a life you enjoy. Enjoy. The little dog looked deep into Rosie's green eyes.

Rosie felt the truth of her words and hugged her close. "Do you really think that? Is she gone?"

No. No. She is not gone forever. She feeds on your fear. She waits. I think Steve and George surprised her and strengthened you. Enjoy while you can. While you can.

George had called her every night since they had returned from Bohicket. He loved to talk, and she enjoyed listening to his deep voice and corny jokes. They had been out on a couple of dates, keeping it almost platonic as they grew closer and closer as friends and soul mates. She really wanted to jump his bones but fought to keep her desires to herself. She often chided herself for falling into Steve's arms so quickly. She was old-school enough that sex meant more than just a roll in the hay. Rosie did admit to herself, and to Hades, that the few nights with Steve had done more for her self-esteem than a hundred hours in a doctor's office.

Chick called her later that night to let her know that she would be out of town for Thanksgiving and she hoped Rosie would be with Gee for the holiday. Chick went on, "You know William and Sara are taking their family on a cruise." Rosie did not know that. "So you will be alone with that happy, kind old lady." Chick gave a laugh, and Rosie groaned.

"Thanks a lot! That's next week, and I did have plans with George." Rosie's voice sank, but she knew she would carry the flag for her siblings. "OK, OK, I will do it. Have a good time wherever it is you are going. And bring me a sercy."

"A what?"

"You remember. A sercy, a gift, a little surprise. Great Aunt Dorothy used that word. You are getting old!"

"Oh, yes," and Chick hung up.

George was very disappointed, as he had planned several surprises for the holiday, including a luxury hotel room, already booked, downtown. Another surprise was going to be cooking steaks on the beach over a fire. And then he would take a deep breath and tell her about a couple of his hobbies. He had not mentioned his hobbies because they were a little out of the mainstream and he did not want to cause Rosie to think he was a perv...he was not a perv, just a little strange.

However, he said he would spend some time with his parents, who lived a few miles out of town and complained they never saw him. He would enjoy his mother's Thanksgiving meal and have a good debate with his father over football. But all in all, it was a letdown.

Rosie packed a basket of little things to take to Ada. She put in many small bags of M&Ms, some Nabs, and several half pints of Jack Daniels 90-proof. Ada would love this, and Hair Weave need not know.

Rosie managed to get to Ada's room without looking at the withered faces she passed. The Hag made a slight attempt to cloud the day, but the stronger Rosie pushed her away and stepped into Ada's room with a little pep. Ada was thrilled to go through the basket. After pouring Rosie and herself a little snort, Ada quickly squirreled the bottles away in her bedside table. Rosie spread a white shawl over Ada's knees. Ada wore the same green dress with white polka dots.

With Rosie pushing Ada's chair, they made the trip to the large dining room, where Thanksgiving decorations adorned each table. The smell of turkey and dressing was delightful. It was strange, Rosie thought, that they made it through the whole very good meal without a mean or snide remark from Ada. Ada even gave Rosie a compliment on her dress. *Is she sick?* Rosie wondered.

Never fear, the dart was always loaded, and just as Rosie turned the chair down Ada's hall, Ada reached out and patted Rosie's arm. "You have beautiful skin," Ada said as she looked over her shoulder at Rosie. "Just a shame you have so much of it." Tears sprang to Rosie's eyes. She froze right there, letting the wheelchair roll on by itself with

Ada, who kept talking. Quickly Rosie gathered herself and stepped up to the chair.

After a little rest, Rosie suggested they go for a short ride around town. Ada was all for it. Rosie got Ada back into her chair and wheeled it up to the front door, which opened onto a lovely porch where several inmates were rocking and sunning in the cool afternoon air. Rosie left Ada and went to get her car. Then she helped her arthritic mother into the front seat. It took several tries to get the eight-hundred-pound wheelchair to fold up and be tucked away in the car trunk. At last Rosie slid behind the wheel and couldn't help scratching off at full speed down the long driveway. Ada gasped, and her daughter smiled.

They rode around the little town with its circuitous streets and huge old oak trees dripping moss from their limbs. They had done this tour several times a year for the past two hundred years, or so it seemed, but it was new to Ada each time. Pointing to a very large old wooden house, Ada told Rosie that was where Joan Crawford had lived in her Pepsi-Cola days and that the long white house over there was where some of the DuPont family used to come for the summer.

When they drove into town, Rosie suggested they stop at a little place and have dessert and a drink. Rosie parked right in front of the bar and went through all the steps of getting Ada out and rolled into the cozy diner. There was a bar up front with a couple of men enjoying drinks and a few tables where people were eating. It was getting late in the afternoon, so Rosie picked a spot where some sun rays still fell on the tablecloth.

An old man with a gray beard took their orders. Ada ordered a chocolaty pudding dish and bourbon on the rocks. Rosie got a white wine. Ada liked the jivy music that was blasting and sort of moved with the rhythm in her chair. She raised her hands and snapped her gnarled fingers, moving her head from side to side with the flow of the music. Her feet tapped a little. She looked happier than Rosie could remember. Drinks consumed and pudding poked at a little, Rosie began to gather their things to leave. The old waiter came back and slapped a large bourbon on the rocks in front of Ada.

"Your boyfriend at the bar sent you this." He nodded toward an old gent at the end of the bar, who nodded in Ada's direction. "He said you got spunk. He likes spunk." Ada raised the glass to the man at the bar and downed half the contents. She continued jiving in her chair.

"You got a drink!?" Rosie was dumbstruck. "A man bought you a drink! That has never happened to me." Rosie could not get over this. "You are ninety-two years old, for God's sake."

Ada just smiled and finished her drink with a flourish. "Time to go or I'll miss my nighttime nip and supper."

Rosie again gathered their stuff and began to push her tipsy mother out to the car. Two men from the bar ran up and offered to help with the loading. Rosie opened the trunk and the car door. With much giggling, many thank-yous, and lots of waving, Rosie and Ada headed out.

It was about a twenty-minute drive back to the house of the living dead. Rosie asked Ada if she had enjoyed herself. Ada gave a resounding yes and allowed her head to fall onto the headrest of her seat. Rosie kept chatting about what they had seen that afternoon and got only grunts in reply. Ada's head moved and rested on her chest, and Rosie heard a couple of snores.

She turned into the drive to the home and noticed the rocking chairs were still busy. She parked right in front of the porch and fought with the bear of a wheelchair until it was ready for Ada. She opened Ada's door, and her mother fell flat out of the car, dead as a doornail, spread-eagle dead, right there in front of God and the chair rockers. The rockers began to call for help and flutter around in shock. Rosie looked at her mother and gracefully fainted away.

Christmas Again

2015

The front door to her condo closed, and Rosie sighed, resting her head on the cool front of the refrigerator. As a child Rosie had found the hum and size of the fridge, or icebox, as her mother had called it, very comforting. She had liked the rumble of the motor turning off and on, especially in the night. It was now two weeks since Ada had died, and Rosie needed comforting. Her last visitor had just left, and the silence was nice. Now she was really alone.

Rosie barely remembered the past weeks. They had been a blur of family and friends, of coming and going and never-ending paperwork. William had done most of the paperwork while Rosie and Chick cleaned out Ada's room at the home. They had found a surprising number of Jack Daniels bottles way back in the closet. The grandchildren had been loud, uplifting distractions. There had been a service at the home for Ada that was well attended. George was always there, quietly, to hold Rosie and give her strength. Now the rush was over. Everyone was gone, and Ada would become a funny family memory.

They would not speak until months later of her ability to inflict pain and hurt that lasted for lifetimes.

Rosie spent the rest of the day straightening her home, which was a mess of clutter—dirty clothes and containers of dying flowers. The mail basket was overflowing, so Rosie decided to tackle that first. Bills, ads, sympathy cards, and one postcard. The card had a very colorful picture of a tree and the ocean. She turned it over and found it was from Steve. Steve! He had not crossed her mind in weeks.

Hades picked up on her tension and dashed over before she had read it. She smelled the boat and a bit of Jigger on the bright card. *What does it say? What does it say?*

"Oh, give me a chance to read it." Rosie smiled at the little dog.

Rosie was thrilled and scared to read the note from Steve. She put the card, picture-side up, on the little table by her chair on the deck. Then she poured a big glass of wine and went back to sit on the deck. She slowly turned the postcard over and read it.

She was stunned. She read it again. He would be at Bohicket between Christmas and New Year's. He wanted to see her. Please be at the condo.

Hades was also stunned. *Will Jigger come? Come? Let's pack right now.* Rosie whirled around in a little dance on the deck, and Hades tapped after her. The wine in her glass flew out and into the chilly wind.

She had not thought about Christmas. Last Christmas had been so much fun, but this Christmas would be different. No Ada, no mother—it hit Rosie hard then that her mother was gone. The fire-breathing dragon had been put to rest. She had always felt that the older generation held the younger generations on the earth, held them down and kept them from floating off into the unknown. Now there was no defense against the murk of life.

No, stop that way of thinking, or you will wake up the Hag. Stop now! Rosie stopped short. Oh, Christmas was in two weeks. Just two weeks to plan and get ready. She had to do something!

Rosie got busy. George came over and helped her. They put out the few decorations she had left and hung twinkling lights from her deck. They always had something to talk about and always found something that drew them closer and closer. After many phone calls back and forth to her children, to her brother and sister, Rosie found that she would rather stay home by herself than go to Disney World with Polly and the boys or go hiking with Star and her new beau, and God knows she did not want to go the ends of the earth to see Izzy. All three of her children were very sweet and made sure she knew she was wanted, but no thanks, darling. Her sister had taken off for California right after the funeral, and William was taking his family skiing for the holidays. She was welcome to come along. Again, no thanks.

Rosie had gotten an OK from William to use the Bohicket condo for Christmas. Rosie thought she and George would really enjoy that and really get close. Maybe they would even check out those thumbs. Now there was this, this card and its implications. Rosie pulled her little dog close and began to think. If she saw Steve, she knew she would have fun—just the thought got her wet. Maybe she would sail off with him for a while, meet fun, interesting people, get real tan all over, see different places. However, she was old enough to know fantasy dreams soon burst. He would spy some interesting woman, and she would be flown back home alone. It would be a real experience, but it would end in hurt.

Now George, on the other hand, offered security, stability, and probably boredom after a while. But he was here and kind and had those big thumbs. The two of them seemed to share something more than the fact that he had gotten rid of her nasty husband—they had similar souls. Rosie told George all about her life, except for the Hag. She covered that by saying she was often depressed. Neither did she tell him that she and Hades communicated. He, on the other hand, always seemed to start to tell her something serious but then ended up making a joke.

"Oh Hades, can you believe that it was only two years ago I got you and I was in a deadly fight with the Hag over my mind? And you saved me?" Rosie asked.

No, you and that floating dick at Bohicket saved you.

"Hades! I thought you liked Steve. What a way to talk, you bad dog," Rosie said.

No disrespect meant. He was a little cocky and sure of himself. Even Jigger told me that. But he was just what you needed to make you strong enough to...to...to live.

"I have never heard you say so much at one time. Oh Hades, what to do? What to do?" Rosie cried.

Just then Rosie's door chime rang out. She ran to the door and opened it to find George standing there with a Santa hat on and his arms full of brightly wrapped packages.

"Oh my gosh, come in, come in. What is up with you, my big, tall Santa?" Rosie gushed.

"I know it isn't Christmas yet, but I have a few things for you." George dropped the packages on the floor and took her in his long arms. "Thought we could get ready for Bohicket."

Rosie's stomach lurched to her feet. Bohicket.

He sat on the sofa, picked up the biggest package, and held it out to her. "Open this one first." He was so excited.

She pulled off the ribbons and the gold paper, flipped the top off the enclosed box. Inside was a vintage, lacy, light blue nightgown. She lifted that out to find a light blue matching negligee with white feathers around the neck and sleeves. Her first thought was *Oh God, I will never fit in that!* Then she saw both were marked "XL," and she smiled.

"George," was all she could say. "George, they are so beautiful. Can I put them on?"

"Please do."

She hurried into her bedroom, stripped off her sweatshirt and jeans, and let the smooth, satiny gown slide over her skin. It fit! She twirled in front of her mirror and slipped on the negligee, twirled again, and called out. "These are so glorious."

She swirled back into the living room and fell to her knees in laughter as big, wonderful George stood there in a matching teddy, black seamed stockings, and huge blue stiletto heels. He even wore a matching light blue garter belt. "Oh Jesus!" was all she could say.

"This is what I have been torn with fear on how to tell you. This is my hobby, my secret." His face was flushed with anticipation of acceptance or fear of rejection. "I decided it was easier to show you than to try to put it into words."

Rosie tried to stand up, but the waves of giggles and laughter kept her on her knees.

"I am not a pervert—I'm not. I just love the feel of the material. I got hooked as a boy." He managed to stand up and pulled Rosie up. "When I was a child, I spent the night at a friend's house, and his mother came in and kissed us good night. We were in bed, and she bent over my face to kiss him. Her nightgown was silk, and it brushed my face. Oh God, that gown felt so good!"

Rosie was not sure what to think. She fluffed the feathers around her neck and straightened the gown. He snapped a garter and looked at her with his big brown puppy-dog eyes. Her knees began to go weak again. She wobbled over to the sofa, still chuckling. Never had she even imagined something like this. *Is he crazy? No, I don't think so*, she thought. She could hear Hades, the Hag, and her mother all shouting, "RUN! Now—run." *Listen, sister*, she told herself, *you are widowed, overweight, not very beautiful, and well over fifty. You can float out to sea for a few weeks or take a chance on this tall, light blue, darling man right here in your home.*

"Pour us some wine," Rosie gasped at last. They consumed several glasses of red wine as he told more of his story, which included more than she had ever wanted to know about nightgowns and vintage undies. He assured her she was the first and only person to know about his hobby. He was shy about it. They stood up and held hands. Then they kissed.

As they held hands and danced around the room, she noticed the old wives' tale was absolutely true. He was absolutely huge, a beautiful column of absolute pleasure. The idea of boredom vanished. On the deck a knowing Hades picked up the postcard and slid it between the rails until a breeze blew it down the creek and into a brilliant sunset.

CPSIA information can be obtained
at www.ICGtesting.com
Printed in the USA
BVHW031358200622
640190BV00013B/364

9 781685 153113